Bigfoot in Tawas

Other books by Madison Johns

Coffin Tales Season of Death

Agnes Barton Senior Sleuths Mystery Series
Armed and Outrageous
Grannies, Guns and Ghosts
Senior Snoops
Trouble in Tawas
Treasure in Tawas
A Cajun Cooking Mystery
Target of Death

Kimberly Steele Novella
Pretty and Pregnant

Agnes Barton/Kimberly Steele Cozy Mystery
Pretty, Hip & Dead

Stand-alone Romance
Redneck Romance

Dedication

I dedicate this book to all of my readers who have stuck by my series and have made Agnes and Eleanor a part of your lives. Thanks!

I love my readers and held a contest in March when I released Target of Death, and the following readers won a spot as characters in Bigfoot in Tawas: Gina Maples Mashai, Sheryl Lynn, and Pamela Ann Tucker.

Bigfoot in Tawas

Madison Johns

Bigfoot in Tawas
Madison Johns
http://madisonjohns.com

Disclaimer:
This is a work of fiction. Any similarity to persons living or dead
(unless explicitly noted) is merely coincidental.

Cover by http://www.coverkicks.com

Edited by Judith Beatty

Proofreader Cindy Tahse
http://www.smashingedits.com

Interior Design by Geoff Brown - Cohesion Editing
www.cohesionediting.com

Chapter One

"You want us to do what?" I asked.

Eleanor shuffled her feet. "I think he just said that he wants to hire us, Agnes."

"Yes, I got that part, El. I just need to hear it again to make sure I heard him right."

Billy Matlin scratched his balding head. "You're Agnes Barton the private investigator, right?"

"Yes, and this is my partner, Eleanor Mason," I said as I thumbed in her direction.

"Okay, well, like I just said a minute ago, I was hoping you could help me find Bigfoot. He's on my property. I just know it."

"Oh? And how can you be so certain?"

Billy went to his roll top desk and returned with a plastic baggie filled with brown hair. I stared through the baggie like I was some kind of CSI, mentally thinking of a lab that might do a DNA check. "How can you be so sure it's Bigfoot and not a dog?"

"Or coyote," El volunteered. "Might be a bear, or not. Hopefully not."

"I've been feeding him, too."

"Like how?" I asked, baffled beyond belief.

"Well, you see ... I take a pizza box and load it with food and then the next day—" He clapped his hands, startling both of us. "The food is gone."

"Okay, so not only are you feeding Bigfoot, but he seems to eat what you leave?"

"That's right."

I just had to ask. "What kind of food does he like?"

"Chinese and Mexican are his favorites."

That made my tummy rumble. "Okay. Would you care to show us about where you put the food? It might help us locate him faster that way."

His brown eyes lit up and he led the way out his back door and into the woods. "Be careful, Eleanor," I said. "Don't trip on a stick."

"Don't trip on a stick?" Eleanor mocked. "Sometimes I think you think I'm five."

"Sometimes you act—" I sniffled as a foul odor drifted into my nostrils. In all of my years as an investigator, I couldn't quite put my finger on the district smell exactly, but it sure smelled like dirty feet for one, and maybe also a wet dog. Since it had just rained the night before, I figured that the woods were simply wet.

"What is that smell?" Eleanor asked me.

"It's Bigfoot, like I told you," Billy said, leaning his scrawny body close to mine.

I smiled kindly, but the odor of the man about blew me over. That had to be where the smell was coming from. I nodded, not daring to speak right now since I'd have to breathe in more of Billy's foul odor.

Eleanor strode straight ahead, not the least bit intimidated, but I knew that was all an act. She just liked to show me up, and since I was lagging behind, she no doubt was trying to show me up. Eleanor came to an abrupt stop and I plowed into her back. "What on earth?" I sputtered.

Eleanor pointed to a pizza box that was near her flip flops. "Is this the pizza box?"

I stared at it with a raised brow. "It sure looks like a pizza box to me, but the strange thing about it is that it's a Jet's Pizzeria box. And we don't even have a Jet's Pizzeria in town."

Eleanor rolled her eyes. "If that is your version of being cute, you'll have to try harder to lighten this situation."

"Oh, and what situation is that?"

"That we have possibly found the dining room of Bigfoot. We'll be on all of the news channels for sure now, and not because we did something dumb."

"Speak for yourself," I said as I whisked a strand of my gray hair back. I then leaned in and whispered, "I sure hope you were joking."

Eleanor stood erect as she gazed through the pine trees up ahead. Her bottom lip protruded slightly and she backed away. "Last one in the car is a goose." She hobbled away and I just stood there shaking my head—that was until the foul odor became much worse, and the bushes ahead of me began to shake. I clasped one hand against my chest and was in such a panic that I just couldn't move. Then a raccoon scurried out and approached the pizza box, gave it a sniff and darted away, all in a span of thirty seconds. I turned to tell Billy how he had it all wrong about Bigfoot eating from the pizza box, but he was nowhere to be seen. Seriously? I grumbled as I strode back to Billy's house. I pounded on the patio door until he opened it and let me inside. "It's safe to say that Bigfoot isn't eating from that pizza box; a raccoon is."

"Oh, is that how your investigations usually go? I had no idea you gave up that easily. You had to have seen Bigfoot in the distance. The way he shook those bushes, it scared the bejeus out of me."

"Is that why you ran off then? If you had stayed longer, you'd have seen that only a raccoon came out of the bushes. From the way he was sniffing that pizza box, I think he might be your culprit. I'm positive he's the one that has been eating the food you leave out there."

"But what about the brown hair I found?"

I stared at Billy's balding head and was thinking of asking him if the hair had fallen off his own head, but instead said, "Why don't you let me take it. I'll ask Sheriff Peterson to have it tested for me."

"Really? So you believe me then?"

"I didn't say I did or didn't, but I think I should do a further investigation into the matter just to put this matter to rest for the entire town. It's bad enough word has leaked. It might help if you quit talking to the press until I can get a handle on what's really happening here."

"But the folks from the Animal Channel are going to be here tomorrow."

"Call them and tell them to postpone your interview, unless you don't want Eleanor and me to investigate."

I searched his sunken brown eyes for a hint of something, anything that might give me a hint of deception on his part, but he just stood there until he finally said, "I can see your point. There's plenty of time to talk with them later after you find more proof that Bigfoot is indeed on my property."

I smiled and thanked Billy, leaving with the bag of hair he'd found. Once I joined Eleanor in the car, she blubbered, "Sorry for leaving you like that, but I wasn't prepared to actually meet Bigfoot today."

"It's not like he's actually in the woods, Eleanor."

"But ... but."

"But nothing. The bushes shook, but only a raccoon came out. I believe that's what has been eating the food all along."

Her lips trembled. "But, I saw his red eyes in the woods."

"Red eyes—where?"

"In the pine trees. I'm sure they belonged to Bigfoot."

I patted Eleanor's hand affectionately. "Now listen here, El. Bigfoot is not hiding in the woods in East Tawas or anywhere else in Michigan."

"How do you know for sure?"

I sat there for a moment considering that, and replied with, "Because Bigfoot just doesn't exist."

"Maybe you're right, but does that mean we're not investigating the case?"

"Of course we are. I was just telling you not to worry is all. Billy gave me the bag of hair and I'm going to see that it's tested. It's the only way we'll ever know the truth for sure.

"Humph, I can't imagine where we're gonna get it tested."

"I planned to ask Sheriff Peterson if you need to know."

Eleanor outright laughed. "I can't wait to see his reaction when you ask him, but what make you think he'll help us at all?"

"Why wouldn't he?"

"Well, for one, he doesn't care all that much for you."

"Nonsense. Our relationship has improved since we've helped solved quite a few of his cases. I dare say that he depends on our sleuthing abilities."

"Hah, I'll believe that when I hear the man say it. He hasn't ever even thanked us."

I tucked my gray hair behind my ears. "He doesn't have to. It's a given."

I drove straight away to the Iosco County Sheriff's Department in relative silence since I just knew Eleanor thought I was nuts, but she'll see when the sheriff tests the hair that was found.

🐾 🐾 🐾

"You want me to do what?" Sheriff Peterson asked, as he leaned forward in his swivel chair with a clang of metal as the wheels of his chair strained beneath the sheriff's bulk.

I held the baggie full of hair, poised to hand it to the sheriff. "Do a DNA test to see if this hair belongs to Bigfoot."

He smiled and shook his head. "So you've been out Billy Matlin's place, eh?"

"Yes. He hired us, in fact."

Peterson swiped a palm over his dark hair that was quite damp. "For what? To deliver me a baggie full of dog hair?"

"No, to find Bigfoot of course."

Eleanor spoke up and said, "I told her she was nuts, but what do I know?"

He laughed. "Billy Matlin has called me out there already, so spare me the details. He gave me the whole story already."

"I know his story seems odd, but what if Bigfoot really is roaming the woods of Tawas?"

"All I know is that man has been getting folks riled up with his

Bigfoot farce of a story. Sure, he's been leaving it food, which, by the way, isn't smart to do since it might lure an animal you just don't want anywhere near your house."

"Like what?" Eleanor asked.

"Raccoons, for one. Or even worse, a black bear."

Eleanor bit her fist. "I knew it. That must have been what I saw lurking in the bushes, Agnes."

"You said you saw red eyes."

"I'm not sure what I saw exactly, but it scared me, bad."

"Getting back to the baggie, Sheriff. Can you have it tested to see what kind of hair it is?"

Peterson leaned back in his chair. "So you want me to use county resources to test that baggie of hair?"

"Yes, of course. Isn't it your job to investigate suspicious animals roaming around?"

"Not unless it has attacked someone or committed a crime."

"What am I supposed to do with this bag of hair?" I asked as I shook it.

"Beats me, but I can't test it."

I stomped out of Peterson's office, ignoring the snickers of the deputies who stood near the sheriff's office who had obviously heard our exchange of words.

🐾 🐾 🐾

Once we were back in the car, I couldn't think straight. "Maybe I should check with the DNR. They might have some idea how to sort this out," I said.

Eleanor hung onto her big black purse and shrugged. "Beats me, but it can't hurt to check, I suppose."

I whirled from the parking lot and made way onto US 23. I remembered that DNR officers congregated at the Whitetail Cafe, so I made my way onto Newman Street, which had many local businesses situated on either side of the street. I parked alongside the curb and Eleanor and I clambered out.

The plate glass window had a picture of—what else but a whitetail deer—with the name Whitetail Cafe above it in bold letters. I entered and waved at Dorothy Alton who was here with her husband, Frank. In the past, Eleanor and Dorothy didn't see eye to eye, but these days things have gone much smoother.

I scanned the booths and took in the aroma of bacon and eggs cooking on the grill. The cafe was only open for the breakfast and lunch crowd, closing at two in the afternoon. I finally spotted the Department of Natural Resources officers in a booth a few feet from the door, noted by the army-green slacks and gray shirts they wore.

Eleanor fidgeted until I elbowed her ahead of me as we approached the booth. "Sorry to bother you, officers," El started. "But my friend, Agnes, here would like to report a strange animal in the area."

I showed them the baggie with the hair. "I was wondering if you could help me determine what animal this hair might have come from?"

The larger of the two, who moved his plate into the middle of the table, said, "Take it easy now. I'm trying to eat here and would rather not get any of that hair in it. Lord only knows what you have there."

"It's Bigfoot hair, or we think it is. The thing is, we're not sure and wondered if you could test it to determine if it does indeed belong to Bigfoot."

The DNR officers tried unsuccessfully not to laugh. "I see. Well … you see, that's not our job."

"Not your job?" I gasped. "What is your job, then?"

"We're in charge of protecting natural resources and many other things you wouldn't be all that interested in since it's not related to Bigfoot."

The other man put a finger in the air, and added, "Unless someone was planning to kill the beast. Bigfoot isn't considered a game animal, so that would be right up our alley."

I stared at their nametags now. "Is that right, Patrick?" I addressed the larger man.

"Yes, Derek is right. Give us a call if you think that's happened and we'll be all over it."

"But since Bigfoot is not real, I don't suppose we'll be hearing back from you," Derek said with a wink.

I would have liked to give them both a piece of my mind, but it would be a waste of breath. There was just no way anyone would believe Bigfoot was real unless we had something more to go on, so I left with Eleanor hot on my heels.

"That went just as I expected," Eleanor said. "We need to call in the big guns."

"Such as?"

"Ask Trooper Sales what he thinks."

Chapter Two

Ten minutes later, I pulled into Trooper Sales' driveway that was located out of town. He's married to my granddaughter, Sophia, and they have a brand new baby, Andrea. Trooper Sales was outside hanging a flower basket for Sophia, who stood a few feet away spouting off instructions. Bill raised a brow at our approach, and once he had finished with the basket he greeted us. "Hello, Agnes and Eleanor. It's about time you stopped by to see the baby."

I'm thinking he meant, *Thank god you showed up so I can get out of here.* He's been fighting domestication ever since he married Sophia.

We followed Sophia into the house and I stopped Bill from excusing himself. "I was hoping for your opinion, Sales." It was still hard for me to get used to calling Trooper Sales, Bill.

He strode into the living room and picked up his daughter, who was on a blanket batting around her toys. He handed me the baby and I cradled her gently in my arms, sitting on a nearby chair. I didn't bother at this point to show him the bag of hair. One of the reasons was that I left it in the car.

"What if we were to say, oh ... that we came into possession of a mysterious clump of hair in the woods? How would I go about having it tested for DNA?"

He scratched his knee. "I'm lost. What's really going on here?"

"We were hired to find Bigfoot," Eleanor informed Sales.

His brow shot up. "Oh, really? Did you come from Billy Matlin's place?"

"Yes, but the sheriff shot us down about testing the hair, something to do with not wanting to use county money for a farce."

"He has a point. I heard Matlin plans to contact the media outside of East Tawas about his Bigfoot theory."

"Oh, really? Won't the sheriff have to get involved then?"

"He told me he's already been out there and it was nothing more than ramblings of the drunken Billy Matlin. He's quite the drinker from what I know about him."

I cooed at Andrea for a moment then said, "I just can't believe nobody seems to be taking his claims seriously!"

"Can you blame them?" Sophia asked as she set two coffee cups down on the coffee table. "It sounds kind of nuts, don't you think?"

"Actually no, dear. Billy seemed genuinely concerned and interested in finding Bigfoot himself. That's why he hired us—to find him."

Sophia wisped back a strand of her curly brown hair. "So this is your big new case? Finding Bigfoot?"

"That sounds like a great title for a book," El said with a chuckle.

"Or Bigfoot in Tawas," I added. "The Animal Channel plans to do a show called *Finding Bigfoot*." I stirred my coffee, and the scent of vanilla wafted in the air. Oh, just how I liked my coffee, liberally doused with vanilla creamer. "I just don't know how to proceed."

"I'll make a few calls," Sales said. "I have some friends who work for the Zoological Society. They might have some ideas."

I handed the baby to Eleanor to hold, instructing her to make sure she didn't let the baby's head drop. "Agnes Barton, I know how to hold a baby, you know."

I had to laugh. "Of course you do, dear. Sorry. I guess it's a force of habit to remind someone how to do it right."

"Yes," Sophia said. "I had to bite my tongue not to tell you the same thing. Motherhood sure changes things."

I had to agree with that. "Where's your mother been hiding?" I asked Sophia, referring to my free-spirited daughter, Martha.

"She is nursing her wounds since she lost her realtor job."

"I'm sorry to hear that. I'll have to check up on her. She seems content to stay at my Winnebago at the Tawas campground."

"She sure is. There's plenty of the right kind of men there—young ones."

I smiled. Was that ever the truth, and here I thought Martha had changed her tune since she became a grandmother. I should have known better.

We left, and I took Eleanor home and joined her inside where we scavenged up whatever we could find in the kitchen, like Tuna Helper. I had to snicker to myself as Eleanor's fiancé, Mr. Wilson, was known for his tuna casserole, although I do believe it's all the man knows how to make. But since he uses a rolling walker to get around, it's surprising that he can even manage that.

I made my way home not long after dinner because there wasn't anything more worth discussing since I had no clue who I could get to test the animal hair. I made the turn into my drive and my cat, Duchess, greeted me when I opened the door. Her meowing grated on my nerves and I gave her fresh water and food, since her bowls were nearly empty.

"Sorry, girl."

I stared around my house that I had only recently moved into after it had been rebuilt. I breathed in deeply, but instead of my knotty pine walls of before, white walls greeted me. My shoulders drooped a little. The knotty pine they have nowadays just isn't like they had in the olden days. I did pick up the fragrance of hyacinths that I had picked earlier in the day and placed into a vase that was centered on my table.

My fiancé, the hotshot attorney, Andrew Hart, was in Detroit on business and I didn't know when he'd return like always. It bothered me a little that he had been gone so much of late, but luckily, Eleanor and I kept quite busy investigating cases. Andrew had proposed a few months back and we had yet to set a date for the wedding. Incidentally, Mr. Wilson proposed to Eleanor around the same time. Truth be known, I'm not in that much of a hurry to tie the knot. Sure, I've been a widow since my forties when my husband, Tom, died of a heart attack, but does a woman my age really need to walk down the aisle and get married? I'm seventy-two, but I'm just not that much in a hurry. Especially since Andrew and I don't completely see eye-to-eye about my sleuthing.

I yawned and plopped down on my leather sofa. I flipped on the television, listening to the story about—who else but Billy Matlin—proclaiming to the reporter about how he had just hired Agnes Barton and Eleanor Mason to find Bigfoot since the law obviously wouldn't do it. I grimaced. "Oh, great. Duchess, that man is gonna make El and me the laughing stock of the town." Duchess, of course, just sat there giving me that uninterested look of hers. I knew she had more important things to think about, like where the last mouse she brought into the house might be hiding since she never kills the blasted things. Yes, it's business as usual at the Barton house.

Bright and early the next morning, I was at Eleanor's house chillin' on the deck and watching the mist rise off Lake Huron as the sun struggled to peek through the clouds. You really never knew what kind of day it would be until you saw the sun shine.

Eleanor was typing on her laptop at the wrought iron table she had recently bought at an estate sale. It seems she thought herself to be quite the social media whizz, but it sure has helped with our investigations in the past. It also kept her content when Mr. Wilson was busy, which he was of late since his granddaughter, Millicent, was visiting from Saginaw.

"Billy sure can't keep his yap closed," Eleanor said.

I bit my tongue so as not to mention that Eleanor also had that problem. "I saw that on the news. I suspect folks in town think that he's plain loco."

"And us, too, since he blabbed that he hired us. Do you think we should drop the case, Aggie?"

"How can we now? We have a reputation to uphold."

"One that's diminished since we're now looking for Bigfoot."

"I can't say that folks haven't thought us a brick short of a full load either, but I suppose you're right. We haven't dropped a case yet, and we haven't had too many cases where we were actually hired," I pointed out. "Have you found anything online about where we might be able to get that hair tested?"

"No, and it's so frustrating. What about the United States Fish and Wildlife Service? They might be interested."

"I guess it couldn't hurt to ask. Does it say how we could get ahold of them?"

She rattled off the phone number of the office in Alpena, and when I made the call, I was told that someone would meet us later at Tim Horton's to discuss the matter. Once I had hung up, I said, "Well, at least they didn't call me crazy."

"You also didn't say why you were really calling. Endangered species, eh?"

"It was the only thing I could come up with, but maybe I can reason with them and they'll investigate."

"Yes," Eleanor chuckled. "And maybe pigs can learn to fly. We'll be lucky if they don't call the men in white coats to lock us up in the loony bin."

I knew she wasn't too far off, but we had to do something. "We could always talk to Leotyne Williams. She's been helpful in the past."

"That gypsy? Oh, what the hay. It's worth a try."

I waited in the car as Eleanor locked up, and once she was settled in the passenger seat I had to ask her, "Are you sure you want to continue on this case, Eleanor?"

"Why suddenly the cold feet, Aggie? I have never seen you back down from a case before, difficult or otherwise."

"I know, but it's so discouraging when we can't seem to get anyone to see reason."

"Oh, phooey. I can't say I really blame Sheriff Peterson for not wanting to test the hair. He has a point. Since the economy took a dive, the county's budget is strapped. Let's not forget that his head would most likely roll if he goes along with us. I mean, what elected official, even the sheriff, would risk his job with something this farfetched?"

"If it's that farfetched, then why are we doing this?"

"To prove to everyone that Bigfoot really does exist."

"The day I get them to believe that is the day I'll wash Sheriff Peterson's police cruiser," Agnes huffed.

Eleanor gripped her big black purse and laughed. "Be careful what you wish for, it might come true."

Instead of responding, I tore off up US 23, heading back into East Tawas and the campground where my Winnebago has been parked for a good while. At least it kept my daughter from living under my roof. She's even more unconventional than I am. She dresses and looks like she was ripped out of the seventies, including that station wagon of hers from the same era. Surprisingly enough, that wagon still runs like a top.

When I pulled alongside my Winnebago, Martha was sitting at the picnic table with a young man who was young enough to be her son, but instead of wasting breath over that, I nodded at the young man. "Hello, Martha. Have you had any luck with finding another realtor job?"

"Nope, I've given up working for someone else. I'm going into business for myself," she said as she strung a bead onto a string. "I'm making jewelry."

"Oh, and where do you plan to sell it?"

"I'm selling it on consignment in the local businesses in East Tawas on Newman Street. Did you know they have a quaint place called Diversions Tea House?"

"You're going to sell jewelry at a tea house?"

"Of course not, Mother. I was thinking we could go there to check out the place."

"They have great bubble tea," the young man remarked as he also was stringing beads.

"What on earth is bubble tea?"

"It's all the rage for the kids these days," Martha said.

"Or young adults," the young man added. "I'm Joshua Crabtree. I met Martha—"

I cut Joshua off. "I'd rather not know, if you don't mind."

"I was going to say at the local tea house. Did you know Diversions has author signings?"

"No, I didn't."

"They have a mystery writer coming for a book signing at Diversions Tea House today. Author Madison Johns, she writes cozy mysteries."

"Cozy mysteries, you say? What on earth is that?" I just *had* to ask.

"He means like Agatha Christie, but not like Miss Marple at all. Madison Johns writes about zany senior sleuths. Very unbelievable, but they sure get themselves into fixes," Eleanor said. "If I didn't know better I'd say the author was following us around and detailing everything we do." She laughed. "She's one of my friends on Facebook."

I didn't like the sound of that at all. "So, what time is the book signing?"

"At noon," Martha said. "So you'll go then?"

"I'm not so sure. I mean, we're on a big case right now."

Martha dropped her beads. "Why didn't you say so in the first place? I'd be happy to help."

"Yes," El began. "We're hot on the trail of Bigfoot."

Martha picked her beads back up. "It's not nice to tease. There's no such thing as Bigfoot."

"Actually, I can't say I agree with that, Martha," Joshua said. "I've seen some pretty strange things near the river."

El's eyes lit up. "Oh, really? Like what?"

I just couldn't keep my lips zipped. "Oh, so suddenly you're a believer?"

"Of course I am, Aggie. Remember I was the one that saw something strange out back at the Matlin place."

"Yes, Billy Matlin, right?" Joshua said. "I heard about that on the news."

I grimaced. "Yes, Billy gave us animal hair that we found, but so far we haven't had any luck finding anyone to test it. We're gonna look up the U.S. Fish and Wildlife Service next."

"Yes," El said in a serious tone. "That is, after we ask Leotyne to look in her crystal ball."

I could just see all of our investigative credentials flying out the window about now.

"Oh, why not," Martha said. "From the way I see it, a little paranormal intervention can't hurt."

Joshua nodded in agreement and I couldn't help but wonder if we were all bat shit crazy. "You don't say. I really expected you to call the men in white coats on us."

"Oh, come on, Mother. It's not like you haven't encountered the paranormal in the past, or used Leotyne's services before. She's a gypsy fortune teller," Martha explained to Joshua.

We made our way across the road to the black monstrosity of a trailer that had all its windows covered with black curtains that you couldn't see through. Martha and Joshua didn't join us, and it was just as well since the trailer wasn't so roomy on the inside.

El knocked on the door and stepped back as a low growling could be heard from inside. I gulped hard and told myself just to calm down lest the hound sense my trepidation.

The door swung open and the black hound bounded down and gave us a quick sniff, then chased a squirrel up a tree. We took that opportunity to climb the few steps that led inside.

Leotyne stood there with hands on hips, dressed in a long black skirt, her long scrawny hair clinging to her head as always. Her olive skin was well wrinkled and her high cheekbones stuck out as her prominent feature.

"I had expected you yesterday," she said as she led us further in the trailer to a covered table where a large globe sat atop a bronze pedestal.

Sitting on a chair was Anna Parson, a battered woman who I had thought had entered the Underground Railroad. "Hello, Anna. I had no idea you were back in town."

"Yes," she shyly said. "I needed a place to stay and Leotyne was kind enough to let me stay with her until I get back on my feet."

"That's great. Is she teaching you how to be clairvoyant, too?"

"Nope, she's already like that," Leotyne said. "She has a raw natural talent that has thus far been untapped."

"I see. Well, I was hoping you might help us with finding—"

"Bigfoot," Anna finished for me.

"Yes. I know how strange that must sound."

She sighed. "Actually, not strange at all. I've had this strange feeling all day and I couldn't quite figure out why until you arrived."

My brow shot up. "Oh, so it had nothing to do with Billy Matlin talking to reporters?"

"Who?"

"If you're clairvoyant, dear, you would already know I was coming and why."

"It's not as clear cut as that, I'm afraid. Sometimes I get feelings that I just can't explain. It's like having a dream you can't quite interpret until it just hits you."

"Okay, then. I have some questions that I'd like an answer to. Like, is Bigfoot real?"

Anna motioned to a chair. "Please, sit."

I did as she asked and she took my hand into hers. Her eyes stared off into the distance and then met mine. She shuddered, her eyes rolled back and she began to sputter. "I can see him in the woods near the river." She wrinkled her nose. "The stench is so overwhelming. It smells like dirty dog and dirty feet."

That got my attention. "Are you sure?"

"Yes, and someone is in grave danger."

"Don't you have to look in the crystal ball?" I asked.

"No, I can see it when I look in your eyes."

"Are you saying that I'm in danger?"

She shook her head. "Not directly, but someone you've met is."

"That could be just about anyone," El said.

"Do you see Bigfoot?" I pressed.

She released my hand. "That's all I can tell you now."

"Leotyne, please. Can't you look in the crystal ball and tell me if you see Bigfoot?"

"Large beasts have been known to walk the earth. Sasquatch in Canada, Skunk Ape in Florida, Yowie in Australia, and yeti/Abominable Snowman in the Himalayas."

"I've heard those stories, but I just have a hard time believing they have merit. I'd have to see this Bigfoot firsthand before I'd believe any such story, but if I could only get someone to test that hair…"

"We'll have to meet with the U.S. Fish and Wildlife Service for sure today and see what they have to say," Eleanor suggested.

"Is there anything else you can tell us, Leotyne?"

She took a necklace out of a jewelry box and placed it around my neck. "Keep this for protection just in case you meet the beast in the woods."

I nodded and glanced at the strange looking figurine. It was brown and looked like an animal of sorts, but not one that I'd recognize so easily. "Thanks," I said, as El and I left.

Once we were outside, I said, "I don't even know why I should believe a thing either of them says."

"Leotyne hasn't steered us wrong before," El said.

"I know, but she's never all that clear either. She speaks in riddles. I have no idea why Anna would ever stay with her."

"Maybe it's just like she said, that she needed a place to stay. Who can blame the girl since that ex-boyfriend of hers battered her."

"I know, but Leotyne Williams is kinda scary to me. There's no way I'd ever sleep under her roof."

"That's because you've never been that desperate."

"Oh, I'm desperate all right. Desperate to solve this case."

"I wonder who might be in danger, Agnes?"

"I have no idea, but we'll figure out something soon, I'm sure. We always do."

Martha and Joshua were waiting for us. "It's almost eleven. We should head on over to Diversions Tea House before it gets much later. I'd rather not be in the back of the line."

"Mystery writer, eh?"

"Sure. It's not every day that we have a book signing in Tawas."

That much was true. We piled in the car and headed for Newman Street. I parked and we headed toward Diversions Tea House and had no problem getting inside. "Hmph, maybe nobody plans to show up for the book signing," I said.

"That's because it's early," a vivacious blond said. She wore a T-shirt that said in bold letters, 'Madison Johns' Number one fan.'

I had to laugh. "Oh, is that right?"

"Yes," the blond gushed. "I'm Gina Maples Mashai. I'm from Texas."

"So you came all the way to Tawas from Texas?"

"No. I'm just here for vacation. Madison's book always made East Tawas sound so inviting that I just had to come to Michigan to check it out."

"We're the Cozy Cats Book Club," a brunette said. "My name is Sheryl Lynn." She pointed out the redhead of the group. "That's Pamela Ann Tucker."

"Where are you folks from?"

"Oh, here and there. It's so exciting to meet Madison Johns finally. I wonder if she's as nice in person as she is on Facebook?" Sheryl Lynn mused.

I replied with, "Is anyone, really?"

"I'm sure she is," Eleanor said.

Pamela Ann Tucker seemed to be the silent one of the group, but she had the most radiant smile. I still didn't know what to do so we went and ordered a tea. Once it was handed to me, I cradled my chai tea gently in my hands and wondered just why I was even here. I admired the place with its built-in shelves that displayed clay teapots and infusers. They had a green counter where you could open up tins with loose leaf tea so you could smell the blends. Their staff was on hand to assist customers with their selections.

Eleanor opened a tin and took a whiff. "This is like being in a candy store, but better since many teas have such health benefits."

"I suppose, but I'm not that much of a health nut. Ginger tea, for instance, is way too strong for me."

"Have you tried green tea?" the girl at the counter suggested. "It has many health benefits."

I nodded. "I'm more of a chai tea latte lover."

That brought a smile to the girl's lips. Her eyes widened when a woman with a gangly young lady wearing a leather jacket walked to the counter and introduced herself as Madison Johns. Madison turned and smiled at us with a nod of her head. She only wore jeans and a simple blouse that you could get off a rack at Walmart, and couldn't be forty—if that. She adjusted her glasses as she was told to set her belongings at a far table.

"Wow, she sure seems nice," Eleanor remarked. "I wonder if that girl is her daughter."

"Or partner," I said. "Hard telling, these days."

Eleanor nodded. "From the looks of that girl, I'm guessing daughter. She doesn't seem all that happy to be here."

"Teenage angst, no doubt."

Martha didn't hold back and introduced herself to Madison. Instead of acting mad about the interruption, Madison shook Martha's hand. Martha motioned El and I over and we exchanged names.

"My mother and her friend, Eleanor, are quite the sleuths in Tawas."

Madison smoothed back her short spiked hair. "Is that, right? How exciting. Have you ever been arrested?"

"Why ... do you ask?"

"I can bet the sheriff wouldn't like to have two senior aged ladies to investigate, was my thinking. At least that's how I like to portray my characters."

"You got that one right. You might want to portray characters in a better light. Like, do your sleuths act all frail since they're senior citizens?"

"Not at all. They even have boyfriends."

El clapped her hands. "I love it."

"This is my daughter, Andrea."

"Hello," I said. "I have a granddaughter named Andrea."

"What a small world. I'd love to chat with you gals in a more relaxing atmosphere and I'm not all that much of a teetotaler, if you catch my drift."

"So you like alcohol, then?"

"Sure do. Would you girls like a signed copy of my book?"

Madison then took our names and before we even knew it we had purchased a signed book. I left and began questioning the help. "Have you heard the stories of Bigfoot circulating in town?"

The blonde with the name of Mandy displayed on her nametag shuffled her feet. "Yes, crazy, huh?"

"I'm not sure. Stranger things have happened in town before."

"Have you ever seen anything that resembles Bigfoot before?" Eleanor asked.

"Actually ... yes. There's a couple of hunting camps behind the Iosco County airport. Now, mind you, behind that is a swamp and woods that lead all the way to the Au Sable River. Anyway, I was with my boyfriend, Bobby, and we were messing around, you know."

"I don't think I do. What do you mean?" I asked for clarification.

"We were out there goofing off."

"And smoking a little reefer?" El asked.

Mandy snuck a glance at the manager who walked into the back. "Yes, but I swear there was something out there with us. There was a horrible smell, and..."

"Did it happen to smell like a dirty dog and feet?" I asked.

"Yes, how did you know?"

"Because I smelled the same thing out at the Matlin place."

She sighed. "Anyway, we heard a strange noise like a whooping noise. I've never heard anything like it before. It scared us so bad that we left and I haven't gone back since."

"So, you didn't actually see anything, then?"

"No, but just thinking about that noise is enough for me to say that Billy Matlin might not be crazy, after all."

"How can you be so sure it wasn't a coyote?"

"I've heard them before, and it didn't sound anything like that."

"But you never visually saw anything?"

"No."

"How about any footprints?"

"We didn't stick around to find out. Word has it that Billy Matlin's neighbors might have seen Bigfoot, too. You might want to check that out. Sorry I can't be of more help."

"You were plenty of help, Mandy. Thanks."

She went back to work and the Cozy Cats book club stared at Madison Johns like she was Mick Jagger, which was weird as heck. We didn't stick around to find out how many people showed up. I was hot on the trail of Bigfoot. I was more than convinced now that Bigfoot in Tawas had to be more than just the ramblings of Billy Matlin. Not that I had any proof, mind you. I just had a feeling, and I had to figure out our next move.

Martha and her friend, Joshua, stayed behind since Newman Street was only a skip and hop from the Tawas campground. I'm still not sold on the idea that the young man was just helping her make jewelry, but I wasn't all that concerned at the time since El and I were supposed to meet someone from the U.S. Fish and Wildlife Service at Tim Horton's.

Chapter Three

El and I soon were making way for Tim Horton's, and once we were in the lobby, I found the U.S. Fish and Wildlife Service investigator easy enough. Not so much by his uniform, but by the crew-cut hairstyle that I knew most investigators had.

I approached a man in jeans and T-shirt. "Are you with the U.S.—?"

He cut me off as he said, "Please have a seat."

El and I sat opposite him. He was tall. I could only estimate at least six feet tall since his legs were folded beneath the table. "I'm Agnes Barton, and this is Eleanor Mason."

At this point, he didn't even take out a notebook or pen. "I gathered as much from the phone call, but what did you have to report?"

"Well, we have some animal hair here that I'd like to have tested," I began as I handed a baggie to him.

He eyeballed the bag, but he didn't take it. "We're not in the habit of testing random animal hair, unless it's associated to a crime that involves an endangered species."

"I see. Well, what do you constitute a crime exactly?"

"Property and livestock damage, or poaching. Do you have anything to report that fits that description?"

I stared into the man's steel gray eyes. "Well, no. I mean not yet. What kind of proof do you need?"

"Dead livestock or endangered animal carcasses. Do you have any evidence of that?"

"Can't you just test this hair?" I implored.

"It doesn't work like that, as I've already said. It has to be the scene of a crime." He raised a brow at my baggie stuffed with hair. "And we'd have to collect our own samples."

I snatched back the baggie. I was madder than a wet hen. "Fine. I guess I'll have to check out the area again. If we find the evidence you're looking for, how can I reach you?"

He handed me his card and stared at the name. Special Agent Duane Dillard. "Thanks. We'll be in touch."

🐾 🐾 🐾

Once we were back in the car, Eleanor asked me, "Why didn't you mention anything about Bigfoot?"

"Because I didn't want that man to think we're nuts. Besides, once he sees the animal carcass, he'll be more than justified to launch an investigation."

"What carcass?" El asked.

"The one we're going to plant, of course."

"Like as in an endangered species?" When I nodded, Eleanor laughed. "How on earth do you plan to do that? It's not like this is the Upper Peninsula and we have a Canadian Lynx running around."

"Of course not, but we do have bald eagles and I spotted a carcass laying on US 23 near your place."

Eleanor's cheeks puffed up. "You can't be seriously considering scraping an eagle carcass off the side of the road, can you?"

I slammed on the gas, and said, "If there's anything left that hasn't been picked clean by the turkey vultures."

I drove to where I had seen the eagle and veered off the side of the road. I waved my arms until the vultures lazily flew away. I then opened the trunk, and pulled out clothing that was in the truck that I had intended to drop off in a Goodwill bin.

Eleanor followed me. "You can't be serious. You're really going to pick up that dead thing?"

"Yes, of course. We need it to get the U.S. Fish and Wildlife Service involved in this case."

"It smells, and probably has maggots by now." She swiped a

hand in an attempt at bating flies away that swarmed near the dead bird. "I hope you don't expect me to pick that thing up."

"I'll do it, but be a dear and body block me would you, so oncoming traffic doesn't see what I'm doing."

Eleanor held out her arms and swayed her body as a truck passed, but instead of traveling past, it pulled off the road. Two men then exited the vehicle and approached us as I tried valiantly to conceal the bird in the shirt.

"Agnes and Eleanor," Curt Hill said. "Is that you?"

His brother, Curtis, smiled with a raised brow, "What do you have there?"

I tried to hold the carcass from their view. "Nothing. You boys should just go along and mind your own business."

"Our ma would be awfully mad if we didn't at least help you out," Curt said. "Whatever it is can't be all that bad or illegal."

Not compared to their activities in the Michigan Militia, no doubt, I thought and sighed. "Only if you promise to keep it to yourself and not laugh."

Curtis folded his arms across his broad chest. "This I have to hear."

I showed the men what was left of the bald eagle. "See, there's nothing illegal about picking up road kill, is there?"

Curtis scrunched up his face as he choked out, "I guess not, but why in tarnation would you want to be doing that!"

"Why do you even care? Don't you boys have your own illegal—"

Eleanor cut me off, and said, "Agnes means I'm sure you boys are too busy to be worrying about what we two are doing."

"We're not worried," Curt began, "but I'm sure curious."

"Fine, then. We're trying to get the U.S. Fish and Wildlife Service out to Billy Matlin's place to test animal hair that we believe might belong to Bigfoot, but—" I never got more out as both Curt and Curtis backed off and strutted back to their big, red, redneck-looking truck, and left us sputtering in the dust as they tore off.

"Well, I'll be," I started.

"Obviously, those boys think we're about as nuts as Billy Matlin."

"Is that how you see it, Eleanor? That Matlin is off his rocker?"

"I'm not sure, but you might want to pick up more of those eagle feathers if you plan to convince that man back at Tim Horton's that an endangered species was poached. But is a bald eagle even an endangered species, Aggie?"

"I don't think so, but I do believe that they're still highly protected." I picked up the remaining eagle feathers and concealed what I had found in the trunk of the car.

Once I was behind the wheel and Eleanor was beside me, I tore away from the side of the road and headed to Billy Matlin's place.

Chapter Four

When I jerked the steering wheel into Billy's place, he was gone. "This might work even better," I said. "No witnesses."

Eleanor's face had been puffed up since we left US 23. "What's up with you?"

She jumped from the car when I stopped, sputtering, "Oh, thank God. I was dying for a breath of fresh air."

"What on earth?"

"Sorry, but Aggie, you smell like decomposition."

"You watch too much CSI Miami," I said as I retrieved the animal carcass from the trunk and made my way for the woods behind the Billy's place. I found a rusted hood from a truck beneath the jack pines covered in dead needles, and scattered the bald eagle's carcass, kicking needles atop it so that it would not look planted and look like it might have been here for a while.

"I guess that's it. All I we have to do now is to call Special Agent Dillard back and report our findings."

"Who?" El asked.

"The man from fish and game that we met at Tim Horton's."

"Okay, but you might want to get cleaned up first because you smell."

"Point taken, but maybe we should wait until morning so it doesn't seem quite so obvious."

"You mean so it doesn't look like you just planted evidence, because that's what you kind of just did." Eleanor bit her fingernail. "I sure hope they don't figure out we were here making it look like some Bigfoot killed a bald eagle."

"Don't worry, El. I'm sure that they'll just have reason enough to test the hair now."

"He did say that they'd collect their own samples, remember?"

"I remember. That's why I'll simply put that animal hair close by."

"Won't that look a little suspect, Aggie?"

"I don't have much of a choice, unless you happen to see any other hair hereabouts?"

Eleanor glanced around. "Nope, none that I can see with these old eyes. I just don't feel right about doing this is all. Maybe we should just take a look around first, and if we don't see any hair then I guess you can leave what you have. But Aggie, how can we be so sure that hair was even found here? I mean, what do we know about Billy Matlin, other than Trooper Sales mentioning that he was quite the drinker?"

I thought about it for a moment. "I guess you're right, Eleanor, but how else will we ever be sure if that hair belongs to Bigfoot?"

"Bigfoot? For all we know there's no Bigfoot. We have to consider the fact that Billy is just nuts."

"Before we make that assumption, it might be best if we canvas the neighborhood."

"Not too many houses way out here, but doesn't the Cat Lady live close by?"

The mere mention of the Cat Lady sent shivers through my body. She's about as odd as they come. She's also a cat hoarder, thus the name, Cat Lady. We found out not long ago that her real name is Bernice Riley, but personally, I can't imagine calling her anything but the Cat Lady.

El and I left for my house so I could take a quick shower. While I was in the shower trying to remove the remnants the bald eagle's stench from my body, Eleanor kept my cat Duchess quite happy with a serious petting.

Once I was re-dressed in white slacks and a green button up shirt, I sauntered into the living room. I brushed my wet hair and tried to fluff it out, hoping that it would dry fast.

Eleanor glanced around the room. "I love this place, Aggie, but aren't you worried staying here all by yourself since it's nestled in the woods?"

"No, should I be?"

"Well, since you believe Bigfoot is running amuck, what would stop him from coming here?"

I gave this some thought as it made logical sense. "I suppose you're right, El, but we don't know for sure if Bigfoot is indeed anywhere near the Tawas area. Besides, this is Tadium, not Tawas."

"Sure, but it's a stone's throw from where Tadium borders Tawas."

I'd rather not think about it that way. "Sure, and I'd worry if Bigfoot is established in the area, but it's quite possible that Billy is a bit *out there*. Didn't you think you saw something when we went out to Billy's place?"

"I thought I saw two red eyes staring at me through the trees, but I can't be so sure now. Maybe my imagination was playing games with me."

I made a pot of coffee, and said, "You're so wishy-washy, El."

She shrugged. "So what if I am? I'm not ready to be locked up in the loony bin with Billy."

I poured us each a cup of coffee, adding plenty of vanilla creamer in my cup. "I just hope this isn't all a farce on his part. I'd hate to think we've gone this far on the lunatic ravings of a madman."

"Stranger things have happened."

The phone rang and I went to answer it, smiling when I heard my fiancé Andrew Hart's voice. "Oh, Andrew," I said. "When are you planning to come back?"

"As soon as I can, Aggie, but what is this I hear about Bigfoot sightings?"

I then explained to him about Billy Matlin hiring El and me, leaving out the part about how we had just planted evidence.

"It sounds like you have your hands full this time, Aggie, but please be careful. I'd hate for something bad to happen to you before our nuptials." He quickly added, "Or to Eleanor."

I nodded as we said our goodbyes. I sighed as I said, "I sure wish Andrew could be here now."

Eleanor's brow shot up. "Are you sure? He's never been all that enthused about our investigating crimes."

"I know, but this case is different. We've never handled a Bigfoot case before."

"True."

I downed the remainder of my coffee. "I think more than enough time has gone by. I probably should call the Special Agent from the U.S. Fish and Wildlife Service now."

Eleanor finished her coffee, and then said, "Oh, why not, but how can you be so sure that he'll come right away? He might have gone back to Alpena for all we know."

"I guess we won't know unless we make the call, now will we?"

Eleanor shrugged as I made the call. Special Agent Dillard answered right away and agreed to meet us within the hour at the Matlin place.

🐾　🐾　🐾

El and I arrived at Billy Matlin's place and waited for Special Agent Dillard to arrive. Billy Matlin's truck still wasn't parked in the driveway and although I did wonder where he was, I never gave it much thought. It might be better that he wasn't here. I'd hate to think that he'd mess up what I'd tried so hard to stage.

El and I sprang from the car just as Special Agent Dillard pulled into the drive and met him as he exited his vehicle with a camera in his hand. "I figured I'd be hearing from you soon so I hung around town, but I was just about to leave. If you hadn't called me when you did, I'd have been long gone."

I'm not sure what he was trying to say, since it wouldn't have mattered when I called him, but instead I said, "I'm sure glad I caught you in time." I led him past the pizza box and he asked, "You're not trying to bait an animal are you?"

"Um, this isn't my place. It belongs to Billy Matlin, so how should I know what he's up to?"

We kept moving and I pointed toward where the eagle carcass was. "That sure looks like the remains of an eagle."

He took a picture. "I think you're right, but it sure looks like vultures have had at it."

"True, but that is to be expected, isn't it?"

He nodded. "So, how did you just come across this so easily?"

I tried to make it sound the best I could. "It wasn't easy at all. El and I have been tramping around in the woods for hours."

"Is that how it was?" Dillard asked Eleanor who hung her head.

"Sure, whatever Aggie says. She's the one who found it."

"I see, and what about the owner? Is he around?"

"His vehicle wasn't in the driveway, so I'm not sure where he might be."

Duane's brow shot up. "Do you make it a habit to trespassing on private property?"

I was taken aback at that. "I'm not sure why you mean by that, young man. You told us to give you proof that there was a crime involving an endangered species and we've simply given you that."

"All I see is a carcass that there isn't much left of. Not much to suggest it's a crime scene at all."

"Oh, so you're making up your mind already not to investigate?"

He gave me a look that was less than kind. "Of course not. It's my job to investigate. I just hope that I'm not wasting my time here."

"That doesn't sound very professional at all, but like you said, it's your job. So do it."

His face tightened. "I don't appreciate you dictating to me what my job is or isn't. I'll have to call in a forensics team to search for samples since all the footprints in there are most likely yours, but from the looks of it, the remains have been here for quite a while." He stopped speaking as he knelt down. "Although, I would have expected to find the remains deeper in the ground. Please, tell me you didn't plant evidence here."

I puffed up my chest. "Of all the nerve. Why on earth would I do a thing like that?"

"To get me to test that hair you found."

"First off, I wasn't the one who even found the hair."

"No, I was," a voice from behind us boomed. Billy Matlin stood there with his hands on his hips. "What are you folks doing on my property?"

"Billy, remember you asked us to help you determine what kind of animal left that hair you found?"

Billy's eyes darkened. "No, I hired you to find Bigfoot on my property."

Special Agent Dillard stood up to his full height. "Is this what this is all about? Bigfoot?"

My eyes widened as Eleanor gulped. "We're not sure exactly, but when we found the bald eagle remains we thought it might warrant an investigation."

The special agent rubbed his neck, but he turned and gave Billy a once over. "Are you responsible for killing this bald eagle?"

Billy shoved his hands in his pockets. "Nope, but Bigfoot might have. When you test the animal hair, you'll find out the truth for sure."

"Look," Dillard began. "I'm not out here to determine if Bigfoot is on your property. I'm here to investigate who might have killed an endangered species—a bald eagle, in this case. Perhaps it was you since it was located on your property."

Billy lit a cigarette. "Since when is a bald eagle even still an endangered species? Wasn't it takes off the endangered species list?"

"While bald eagles are no longer protected under the Federal Endangered Species Act, they remain protected under the Bald and Golden Eagle Protection Act. So if you were responsible for killing this eagle, you're in deep trouble. I'm ready to cite you for unlawful animal baiting."

Billy's eyes widened. "For feeding Bigfoot?"

"I'm not all that sure what animal you were trying to bait, but there's a ban for baiting right now."

"No, there's not. I've checked with the DNR—Department of Natural Resources—and they lifted the ban for deer baiting, but I'm not baiting deer. I'm simply trying to prove that Bigfoot is roaming on my property, which you'll know when you test the hair I found. Agnes, give him the hair."

I shrugged. "He told us earlier that he had to take his own samples. We should just let him do his investigation."

Dillard made a call via his cell phone, alerting whoever was on the other end that he needed assistance, rattling off the address. Once he hung up, he told us to wait back at the house.

I was curious as to what the U.S. Fish and Wildlife Service would do investigation-wise, but figured I had better do as we were told this time. As it was, I think he might just smell a rat, but I suppose he had plenty of experience under his belt to realize our staged scene just didn't cut it. El and I had only to stick to our story.

Chapter Five

Once we were settled on Billy's plaid sofa, he asked, "Where did you get that eagle carcass?"

"We found it out there," I said, nearly choking on the lie.

Billy shook his head, "I'm not a fool. I know my property like the back of my hand and it wasn't there yesterday."

"How can you be so sure?"

Billy clenched and unclenched his hands into fists. "I'm not sure how you did it, but you had better spill your guts."

I swallowed hard. "It's road kill. It's the only way we have a chance to get the U.S. Fish and Wildlife Service to test that hair you found."

"What about the sheriff? Can't he do it?"

"He refused to do it, claimed that it wasn't related to a crime. The DNR won't get involved either. This the only way."

"Yes," Eleanor began. "The special agent told us the only way that they'd get involved was if an endangered species was involved."

"Except that he thinks I was the one responsible for that bald eagle's death."

"He'll have to prove it first."

Billy started to pace the room. "Well, it was on my property and that's probably all the evidence they need to arrest me."

"Don't be so melodramatic," I said. "They'll find the hair, and test that before they make any determinations. I'm sure of it."

He stopped pacing. "I thought you said they'd have to collect their own samples? What if they don't find any?"

"They will, because I made sure to drop the hair nearby."

"I just don't like this. Why won't anyone believe that Bigfoot is on my property?"

I wanted to say *because it sounds crazy for one reason*, but instead I said, "Folks just don't believe anything unless they see it firsthand, I guess. Have you taken any pictures?"

"I haven't seen him exactly, so I haven't had the chance to take any pictures."

"You mean to tell me that you haven't set up any game cameras?" El asked, exasperated.

Billy scratched his chest. "I never thought about doing that, but I sure will once the agents leave.

I had serious doubts about Billy's story for real now. He ought to have been smart enough to know that he should have set up cameras. As it was, Billy's elevator didn't go all the way to the top floor.

Headlights illuminated the living room as trucks tore into the driveway, followed by none other than Sheriff Peterson. He didn't go around back, but rapped on the front door.

Billy answered the door and the sheriff came inside, eyeing El and me. "So Billy, what have you gotten yourself into now?"

"Now listen, Sheriff. This isn't my fault. I told you about Bigfoot being on my property, but you only stayed ten minutes discussing the matter with me, and now it must have killed a bald eagle on my property."

"Aggie, what do you have to say for yourself?"

"I told you Billy hired us, and we're trying to find Bigfoot, but since nobody would test that animal hair, we had to find another way."

"So magically a bald eagle carcass mysteriously appeared on Billy's property?"

"I tried it your way. I met with the DNR and the U.S. Fish and Wildlife Service, but I was told the only way they'd launch an investigation was if it involved an endangered species, or at least a still protected one."

"This is a bit much for even you, Agnes. Since when have you two gone into the Bigfoot hunting business? East Tawas doesn't need another frenzy of people traipsing into town looking for Bigfoot."

"Oh, so Bigfoot has been spotted here before?"

"I meant that first it was the ghost hunters and then treasure hunters. When will this madness stop?"

Billy's face became beet red. "Now listen here, Sheriff. I'm not a liar. Bigfoot really is on my property and Agnes and Eleanor are gonna prove it."

"The only thing these two are good for is riling folks up. They should have just told you straight off that they couldn't help you. They're crime investigators, not Bigfoot hunters. If we don't watch out, game hunters will be coming to town."

"I sure hope not, Sheriff," I said. "That sure wasn't my intent. All I ever wanted to do was to get that blasted hair tested."

"Agnes, do you know for sure where it even came from?"

"I gave it to her," Billy spat. "I'm getting so sick of people thinking I'm a deranged fool."

"Then don't act like one. Where did you find that animal hair, really?"

"On the pizza box I've been leaving food on. When it's tested, you're all going to owe me a huge apology."

"I believe you, Billy." I sorta did. "That hair is the key to this puzzle. When it comes back as Bigfoot hair, you'll be vindicated."

"Oh, so they already have Bigfoot hair to compare it to?" the sheriff laughed. "I doubt that very much."

"Why are you so insistant that Bigfoot doesn't exist?" Billy asked with narrowed eyes.

"Well, for one, I've never seen anything remotely close to Bigfoot. Plenty of white-tailed deer, coyotes, foxes, and even a few black bears, but none of them look a bit like Bigfoot. That might just be fox hair. What do you plan to do when they come back with a report that confirms that it's hair from a confirmed Michigan species of wildlife?"

"If it comes to that, I'll apologize, but until then I plan to continue to search for Bigfoot."

Sheriff Peterson threw his arms in the air and stomped outside, heading in the direction of where the bald eagle carcass was. Sure, the sheriff had made a few valid points, but I wasn't about to let him know that. It never even occurred to me that big game hunters might head to town. I sure hoped that wouldn't be the case, but if it was, I'd do anything in my power to stop them from disturbing the habitat of the local wildlife.

We waited a few hours before two men knocked on the back door and were let inside by Billy. Special Agent Dillard approached us with the two DNR officers we had seen at the Whitetail Cafe, Derek and Patrick.

"I thought the U.S. Fish and Wildlife Service were handling this investigation?" I exclaimed as a question.

"It seems there is some dispute over who should handle it," Special Agent Dillard said with a grimace. "I'm sure it will be worked out."

"We're more than capable of handling the investigation," Derek said.

"It's more of a jurisdiction issue, but the U.S. Fish and Wildlife Service supersedes that of the Department of Natural Resources."

"I don't see how. We have just as much of a vested interest here," Derek insisted. "We'll be retaining the evidence you found."

"Not happening. I'm taking it back to Alpena to have it tested, and I'll be happy to give you a report on our findings."

Derek added, "I'll have to call my supervisor before I allow you to do that."

"Allow? I think you're overstepping your authority here, Derek."

This was getting interesting, but going nowhere fast. "Sounds like Agent Neering has a valid point," I said, butting in.

"I'm not interested in your opinion, Ms. Barton," Derek said. "Let us handle our own affairs."

"I came to you first, but you DNR guys blew me off. Special Agent Neering was the only one who told us to find evidence of a crime associated with an endangered species. All you two did was laugh at us."

"Oh, really? Did you also mention you were looking for evidence to support your theory that Bigfoot is roaming the woods of Tawas?"

I ignored Derek's accusation. "No, the truth is that I'm not sure what killed that bald eagle, but we did come into possession of evidence of hair found nearby. Once it's tested, we'll find out for sure what animal might be responsible."

The DNR guys pulled out their cell phones, but by then, Special Agent Neering was already out the door with Derek and Patrick hot on his heels. Neering scooped up a black bag and headed for his vehicle, ignoring the DNR officers as they continued to run off at the mouth that the agent had better let them have the evidence.

Within minutes, Neering had hopped in his truck and tore off down the road.

Sheriff Peterson stomped his way inside and said, "This is quite a mess you girls have caused this go around. Now those fellas are going to be arguing for months over this matter."

My brow shot up. "Months?"

"Well, yes. What had you expected, a quick resolution?"

"I suppose not, but I didn't think it would take months."

"It's no different than any crime investigation. DNA analysis is a lengthy process that will be further delayed as they argue over the chain of evidence. I'm for once glad that I'm not involved."

"Is that why you came back in here, to rub it in our faces?"

"No. I just wanted to caution you all to keep your mouths closed about this matter until the results come back."

"I'm sure you know that El and I plan to continue to investigate the matter."

"Sure, just leave me out of it in the future. I don't even want to hear the name Bigfoot again," he said as he headed out the door.

Billy shrugged. "Is that how you plan to proceed, by downplaying the whole Bigfoot thing?"

I smiled. "I think it might be best until we can gather more evidence. We plan on questioning your neighbors next. I have a hard time believing that they haven't seen anything. We were already given information that someone might have just run across Bigfoot behind the airport."

"I wouldn't doubt that. I can't be the only one who's seen the beast hereabouts. Just stay away from the Cat Lady. She doesn't cotton to strangers showing up at her place," Billy informed us.

"Not a problem. We've known her for years. She really doesn't mean any harm, but I have to admit she's rather quick to aim her shotgun at trespassers."

"That's been my experience with her, too. I've seen her out in the woods a few times, but she's not very approachable, if you know what I mean."

I really did know what he meant. "You do plan to forgo the appointment with Animal Channel, right?"

"You have a week to turn up something, but if you don't find anything in that time, I'm going ahead with that interview. I'm sure excited about getting featured on the Animal Channel. It's not every day that happens to someone like me."

I had to agree with that, but I sure wished I had more time. A week wasn't all that much to find enough evidence. "Just be sure to set up the game cameras. Okay?"

"I sure will, and thanks for the idea. I'm not sure why I hadn't thought about doing that before.

Chapter Six

Once Eleanor and I were back in the car and headed toward Billy's nearest neighbor, Eleanor said, "For a man so insistent on proving that Bigfoot is on his property, why didn't he already have game cameras set up, Aggie? It makes no sense."

I had to agree with Eleanor. "Oh, how should I know? But it sounds like he's going to do it now."

"I just don't know about this case. How on earth are we going to find Bigfoot anyway? And better yet, how are we going to catch him?"

I gripped the wheel and said, "I don't know, but we've already invested enough time in this case. I can't imagine quitting now, just when it's getting good."

"Good how?"

"Well, it's funny to watch the DNR and the U.S. Fish and Wildlife Service fighting over the evidence."

"I wonder how much it's gonna cost us if they found out we planted that bald eagle?"

"There is no way we can ever tell anyone about that, or our goose will be cooked for sure. Keep your lips zipped, Eleanor. And that means not telling anyone, including Mr. Wilson, your intended."

Eleanor shot me a look. "Fine, but that also includes leaving that lawyer man of yours out of the loop, too."

"I can agree with it. I'd be afraid of what he'd have to say about that."

"Nothing good, I'm sure," Eleanor laughed.

I drove down a spell, past more jack pine trees that were in the area. I daresay I had my eyes peeled to the road for more than just a white-tailed deer, like I half expected to see Bigfoot, which was just ludicrous since there was no such thing. Or was there? This case sure had me second-guessing myself. Although I couldn't imagine Billy fabricating an elaborate story such as this, especially when it came to that bag of hair he had found. The origins of the hair did nag at me, though. I guess I'd feel much better about it if I was the one that had found it.

I slowed down when I spotted a mailbox, and rumbled up the pothole-filled drive. I skidded to a stop when a single story house came into view with a very familiar red pickup truck parked alongside it.

Eleanor shook her head. "This can't be—"

Before Eleanor had a chance to finish that sentence, or before either of us had a chance to step a foot out of the car, shotguns were leveled at both of our heads. We raised our hands and waited for Curt and Curtis Hill to realize that it was us before they shot our heads off.

Curtis was the first to lower his weapon. "Mrs. Barton, is that you?"

I bobbed my head profusely. Curt swung his shotgun barrel down and onto his shoulder, waving us out of the car. Eleanor and I cautiously stepped out of the car and I said, "Sorry. I had no idea you boys lived here."

"You can't just whip in here like some kind of badass, you know," Curtis said. "It's just not safe."

"Sorry. I didn't think that I had. It was just that I was avoiding that last pothole. It looks big enough to sink a car."

Curt lowered his head. "We like it that way. That way if the government ever drops by, it will catch them for sure."

"The government? Why would they be stopping by when you boys are law-abiding citizens of Tawas?" Not, not, definitely not!

Curtis chuckled, stroking his beard. "We have been since our last trip to the pen, but that was only for petty crimes."

"It's just that we associate with folks involved in the Michigan Militia, but I'm sure our ma already told you that."

I forced a smile on my face. "Not that I remember. I have heard some talk around town, but it's really none of my business since you boys have always been so kind to me. Why, you even helped me when the awning to my camper fell down." I knew that I was rambling, but I couldn't stop myself. I was so nervous, not that either of the Hill boys had ever given me reason to be.

Curtis stood there, keeping a tight hold of his shotgun. "I'm sure you didn't come here to shoot the breeze, so why did you?"

"Like I already said, I didn't have a clue you boys lived here. Your neighbor, Billy Matlin seems to think Bigfoot lives on his property." I paused to read their expressions, but they both were stone-faced. "What's your take on that?"

Curtis climbed the few steps that led inside. "Come on in and we can talk about it."

El and I followed Curt and Curtis inside, and we walked around a motor that was sitting on a piece of fabric in the middle of the floor. The room was sparsely furnished, with only a brown couch that was ripped on the arms. In the far corner, where you'd expect to see a television or computer, was a ham radio with receivers and a microphone that you could speak into.

I swallowed hard as the walls had a variety of firearms, from rifles and shotguns to semi-automatics attached, and metal boxes filled with ammunition were near the couch. I walked to a table and picked up one of the books, among many, on conspiracy theories. "A little light reading, boys?"

Curt took the book from me and motioned us toward a table near the patio door where we all sat. I gazed through the window and noticed trenches were dug in the backyard. "Planning to expect company out there?"

"Nope. We just do a little training here," Curtis said. "What did you want to know again?"

"Have you seen anything strange in the woods?"

"Plenty of strange things going on around here, if you ask me," Curt said with a chuckle and his brother joined him. "Bigfoot wouldn't stand a chance around here. We'd use him for target practice."

"I see. Well, what do you make of Billy Matlin?"

Curtis leaned back in his chair. "He's a strange one, for sure. I almost shot him last month. He's always poking around in the woods. I have no idea what he's looking for."

"He's looking for Bigfoot, actually," I said.

"No shit, for real?" Curtis asked. "He must be crazier than I thought. Or more than people think we are."

I looked right into Curtis's eyes. "I don't think either of you boys are a bit crazy, not with things like they are now. I can imagine we're all a little sick of the government sometimes."

Eleanor nodded. "She's right. So you've actually seen Billy out in the woods then?"

"Yup," Curtis said. "He was carrying around a baggie and tweezers like he was looking for something. Insects is what I thought, or what he told me."

"Is that what he really said?" I asked baffled. "Why on earth wouldn't he tell you the truth if he's looking for Bigfoot?"

"Probably because of the ten million dollar cash prize offered by one of those reality shows, or so my ma said."

"So.your ma told you that?" I asked.

"Sure did."

"But Billy never told you that?"

"No. He told me he was looking for insects."

"No wonder you almost shot him."

"If he hadn't gotten so close to our place, I wouldn't have bothered him at all.

"And you'd never met him before?"

"No, but I know who he is. I've seen him around Tawas. He's even been out to our ma's potpourri shop. She can probably tell you more about him than we can. I've told you all I know about him."

I gave this some thought. "So neither of you boys have seen anything that resembles Bigfoot?"

"Plenty of big men with beards around, but none that would fit the description of Bigfoot."

"No strange footprint either?"

Curtis gave Curt a look and said, "Actually we did find something strange nearer to the airport. We were canvassing the woods for signs of white-tailed deer and found this strange footprint in the mud. Out of curiosity, Curt did a plaster cast. It's out in the barn."

"Why would you do that if you weren't interested in finding Bigfoot?"

"I wasn't looking for him," Curtis said. "But when our ma told us about that cash prize, we thought that it couldn't hurt to take a look around."

"Can we take a look at it?" Eleanor asked. "I mean, I'm sure it doesn't' belong to Bigfoot, but I'm curious, too."

Curtis got up and we all followed him out the patio door and into a barn that had three locks on it. "Before I let you inside, Mrs. Barton and Mrs. Mason, you have to promise not to relay any information back to Sheriff Peterson, about anything you have seen in our house or inside our barn— agreed?" Curtis said.

"I promise on the life of my daughter, Martha," I said. "Besides, you're the sons of one of our best friends, Rosa Lee Hill."

Eleanor smiled. "Exactly. We can be tight-lipped when we want to be."

Locks were turned, latches thrown aside, and the barn door was opened. I half expected to see a government official tied up inside, but not a chance. My eyes did widen a tad when I saw the gas masks hanging on nails, but there were also generators under tables and canned foods packed on shelves overtop. If the apocalypse ever happens, I'm heading straight here. At least I know a couple of survivalists.

Black plastic hung over a doorway in the back, but I quickly diverted my eyes when Curtis's face hardened. I'm sure this was under the *I didn't need to know* category so I asked, "And the cast would be where?"

Curtis opened a cabinet and carefully set a plaster cast on the metal table. "This is it. What do you think, Mrs. Barton?"

"Please, call me Agnes," I said.

Eleanor smiled. "And just call me Eleanor. It's about time we get better acquainted since you've both been kind enough to share this with us."

I set my hands on either side of the plaster cast in awe. It was at least— "Hey, Curtis. Can you grab a measuring tape?"

Curtis reached in a drawer and came back with one, pressing it into my hand. I pulled out the metal tape and the cast measured twenty inches. Eleanor fingered the cast. "Would you look at it, Aggie? This isn't just a footprint. You can see the toes."

"I see that. When did you take this cast?"

"A few months back. It was way colder then. More than cold enough for that cast to be made. Otherwise, I think it we wouldn't have gotten a good one."

"Whereabouts did you see this again?"

"It was behind the airport. We could show you where, but the trees are very dense in that area and neither of you are fit enough to make the journey," Curt said. "I'd hate for one of you to break a hip or something. It would be awfully hard to carry either of you back out of there."

Eleanor's hands flew to her hips. "I sure hope that wasn't a crack about my weight."

"Not at all," Curt said. "I was just saying you're too old to be going way out there."

Eleanor glared at him and snapped, "We're not old, we're seasoned."

I massaged my right hip. "They're right. We can't go out there. We'll take your word for it that you found this footprint behind the airport. We were already given information that strange things have been seen in that area. How about noises?"

Curtis looked at Curt who shrugged. "We heard this strange animal noise. It sounded like a whopping noise."

"Whopping noise?"

"That's the closest description I can give you. It was eerie, is what it was. Believe me when I say that if that thing had surfaced, I'd have dropped him real quick-like."

"Thanks, Curtis. Is it okay if I take a picture of the cast?"

"Go ahead, but you can't take it with you. We might just have a shot at that ten million dollars yet."

"No visual though?"

Curtis and Curt shook their heads and I had to believe them, because if they had seen anything like a Bigfoot, they'd have shot it dead for sure.

Chapter Seven

The next stop El and I knew all too well. Bernice Riley was known as the Cat Lady and I considered her a friend for the most part. She, like the Hill boys, was a little on the shotgun-happy side. I'd have called her if she had a phone to forgo another round of staring into the barrel of yet another firearm today, but heck, I've never been one to shy away from anyone, crazy or not. Now, I don't exactly consider the Cat Lady crazy, even if she does have more cats than most folks I know of. Eccentric might be more of the word to describe her.

"Hold on now, Aggie," El said. "Don't drive in the Cat Lady's driveway so fast. No sense in startling the old girl. She might just shoot first and ask questions later."

"If she did that, I doubt I'd hardly be able to answer questions." When the car rolled to a stop, my mouth hung open. The Cat Lady's modest abode had gone through a renovation. Her house had a fresh coat of yellow paint and her wrap-around porch had new handrails and floorboards.

"Wow," El said. "I had no idea that the Cat Lady had enough money to renovate. Since when does she have funds enough to do that?"

I shrugged, and El and I got out of the car just as the Cat Lady walked toward us with a wave of her hand. She was dressed in a white button-up shirt, her brown slacks tucked into her knee high boots. The boots were the only familiar part of her wardrobe that I was used to seeing her wear.

"Hello, Cat Lady," I said.

As she neared, I saw the blush on her lined cheeks. It was all I could do not to cross myself. This couldn't be the Cat Lady we've known all these years.

"Please, call me Bernice. It's my real name, you know."

"Since when?" Eleanor asked.

"Since always, silly. Plus, I don't want to sound crazy when the folks with the cameras show up."

I blinked my eyes a few times as they watered up from way too much pollen. I proceeded to clamor up the steps that led to the porch. It was then that I saw the oval of the wood door with stained glass. I turned to face Bernice. "What cameras?

"For that reality show. *Hunting Bigfoot,* silly. They fixed up my place for free, even. They told me my house was deep in Bigfoot country."

"They did? And you didn't run them off the property with your big gun?"

"Sure I did, at first, until they explained that they'd be willing to renovate my place free of charge, plus pay me for allowing them to film here."

"What do you make of that? Bigfoot, I mean?"

"I really don't care one way or the other."

"That sounds like a bunch of baloney," Eleanor said.

"Oh, come on, Eleanor. You had to have heard about what crazy ole Billy Matlin has been saying in the local press. He's convinced that Bigfoot is roaming his property, and he lives nearby. I figure if Bigfoot is on his property, than it's quite conceivable that he has been on my land, too. I have the scat to prove it."

"Scat?" I asked.

"Yes, you know … fecal matter. The kind an animal leaves behind."

"Eww," El said. "That's nasty."

"Brent has been taking samples all week."

I gripped my chin in thought. "Who is Brent?"

"He's the man who will be hosting the show on the Animal Network. He's not half bad on the eyes, either. You'd like him, Eleanor."

"Eleanor is engaged these days," I clarified.

"That doesn't mean that I don't still like to look, Aggie. Is he here now?"

"He left to get more supplies. Come inside. I made a fresh batch of moonshine," she laughed. "I mean lemonade. I gave up making moonshine since Sheriff Peterson almost arrested me not long ago. He accused me of making folks sick, if you can believe that."

I believed it all right. I had suffered my own bout of intestinal difficulties after the last time I had sampled it. "That's good to hear. Jail is no fun."

Bernice led the way inside. Her wood floors had also been redone, and she had furniture that consisted of a striped pattern couch and chairs that were set around her fireplace. There was also a tripod set up with a camera attached, and a few more set up with lights that you might find on a movie set.

I almost wouldn't believe it if I hadn't seen in with my own two eyes. This sure put a spin of realism to the whole Bigfoot thing. At first, I had believed that Billy was bat shit crazy, but now, there was a television crew actually investigating. I was not about ready to let them find Bigfoot before El and I had a chance to. Instead of wondering, I asked Bernice, "So tell me. Have you actually seen Bigfoot yourself?"

Bernice bit her lower lip, and informed us that she'd bring us some lemonade, darting off presumably to do just that. "I don't get it," I said. "Why would the Cat Lady let some stranger to set up right here?"

Eleanor rubbed her hands together. "Unless she's seen something, herself."

"I was trying to ask her before she went for the lemonade. Why is she stalling?"

"I'm not sure, Aggie, but why don't you ask her again?"

I had planned to when Bernice set a tray full of lemonade down, handing us each a glass. I stared at the clear glass with the lemon-colored liquid inside. At least this time around her beverages looked safe enough to drink. I took a sip and the sourness about floored me. "Geez, didn't you put in any sugar?"

"Oh, sorry. I'll get you some." Bernice dashed off and returned with packets of artificial sugar, and El and I both mixed a few packets into our drinks.

"Thanks," I said. "And about Bigfoot?"

"Brent told me I shouldn't talk about that to anyone. To save it for the show."

"Oh, come now. I thought we were friends, Bernice."

Bernice gave me the eye. "I'm not sure I'd say that, but why do you want to know?"

"Because Billy hired me to find Bigfoot."

"Smart move on his part, but what do you know about finding Bigfoot, Agnes?"

"I don't, but El and I sure are trying. Even the Hill boys gave us information."

"I'm just not sure. Brent wouldn't like it, and I'd hate to get him mad since he renovated my place so nice."

"I won't tell anyone you told us. I promise."

"Yes, but there's ten million dollars on the line here."

"Ten million dollars?" El asked with widened eyes. "That sure is a lot of dough."

"So let me get this straight. There's a ten million dollar prize for finding Bigfoot?"

"Yes," Bernice said. "I figured the Hill boys would have told you that when you were at their place."

"They did, but I was just wondering if there was any truth to it. Is Brent paying out the money?"

"I'm not sure who is for sure, but it's the premise for the show."

I had to know what Bernice had seen, so I kept pressing. "Please, Bernice. Have you seen Bigfoot out here?"

"You promise if you find Bigfoot you'll give me a cut?"

"I promise." I might as well promise since Bigfoot might never be really found.

"I've seen the hairy beast out back of my property. I've even seen him scampering across US 23 before."

"Why haven't I heard your story before?"

"Because folks already think I'm nuts. I sure don't want them committing me to a nut house."

"How close did you get … to Bigfoot I mean?"

"About a hundred yards."

"How is your eyesight these days?" Eleanor asked.

"I can see pretty well, Eleanor. All I can tell you is that what I saw wasn't human."

"Have you seen it more than once on your property, or just the one time?"

"I've seen it about three times this month. The other morning, the beast was standing by my oak tree out back. He even left telltale signs."

That got my attention. "Like what?"

"I can show you." Bernice went out the back door with El and I closely behind her. My senses were heightened, too. The wind rustled the limbs of the trees and a hawk circled overhead. A woodpecker was tapping a nearby tree, but as we neared the tree, it became deadly silent. I stared at the tree where three claw marks had broken the bark just as a strange noise carried to where we stood, with a whoop, whoop, whoop. Eleanor and I clung to each other and Bernice's eyes were wide, staring behind us. I was scared senseless, but I had to take a peek. Something or someone ran in the distance, its brown clothing or fur moving as it did.

"It's Bigfoot," El whispered.

I pried Eleanor's fingers from my arm. "We don't know that for sure, Eleanor. I couldn't tell if that was a man wearing a coat, or something resembling Bigfoot."

"It was Bigfoot, all right," Bernice said. "He's been here before. I can almost smell all that cash."

"I'm sure you need more proof. Has Brent set up any game cameras out here?"

"Sure he has, and they always end up getting damaged, like someone or something tore it down. That Bigfoot is way smarter than they give him credit for. I can't wait until the show. When Brent finds the proof, he'll—"

"He'll what? Share it with you?" El asked. "That's a bunch of hogwash. If he finds Bigfoot, he'll keep all the loot himself, is my thinking."

"Eleanor has a point. Have you signed anything that says you'll get part of the money if he finds Bigfoot, or has he just led you to believe that?"

"No, but I assume that he will."

"Assume, hell," El spat. "You need something in writing."

The back door opened and a man with dark hair and a goatee approached us. "What's going on here?" he asked.

"Hey, Brent. My friends Agnes and Eleanor stopped by to visit."

"I told you to stay out of the backyard, remember?"

That got my blood boiling. "Stay out of her own backyard?"

"Yeah, and who made you the boss?" El asked. "Just because you're shooting a reality show here doesn't mean that you run her life."

"Perhaps you should just butt out," Brent suggested. "You have no idea about the arrangement Bernice and I made."

"Oh, but we do," I started. "It seems that you are searching for Bigfoot, but does Bernice get a cut of the money if you find proof that he actually exists?"

"Of course not. I paid to renovate her place. I believe that is payment enough."

"Hogwash," El said. "You Hollywood types are all the same."

"For one thing, I'm not from Hollywood. I'm from North Carolina, and I already have a signed agreement with Bernice. I suggest you leave so we can finish the preparations for the show."

That ruffled my feathers, but I decided to move Eleanor along before she put a serious hurting on this loudmouth. Bernice walked with us to our car. "Sorry, girls. He's right. I already signed the agreement."

I squeezed her shoulder. "Well, the renovations sure spruced up the place, but where are all of your cats? I didn't see any of them here."

"Brent suggested I get rid of them, so I took them over to Elsie Bradford's place for safekeeping."

"Elsie took in your cats? I can't believe it."

"She didn't really want to, but she has all that property and told me she'd make sure they were fed until all of this was over."

I nodded as El and I climbed into the car. I then turned around and headed toward Elsie's place. "All of those cats at Elsie's place. This, I have to see," I said.

Chapter Eight

Eleanor grumbled on the way to Elsie Bradford's house. "I'm hungry."

"Okay, how about I roll into KFC?"

"That sounds great to me, but that place sure hasn't done a thing for my figure," she chuckled. "Not that I worry about a thing like that my age. I'd rather go out with a chicken leg in my mouth than have a salad as my last meal."

"Since when do you talk all morbid? From the way you sound most of the time, you're a spring chicken."

"That's all an act and you know it. I know I'm old, all right. I just don't like it when someone calls me that. I do know how to use it to my advantage if it will get me through a line quicker though. Is there something wrong with that?"

"Not at all. I admit it bothers me that folks much younger than us are dropping like flies lately. We've gone to three funerals in the last six months."

"Don't remind me, Aggie, but they were all heart related."

"Yes, but I still can't believe that there are that many people out there with a disposition to heart disease."

"Another reason we should maybe start watching our food choices—tomorrow. Today I'm ready for a fried chicken meal."

I parked in the parking lot of the KFC, which was more packed than usual, even for lunchtime. El and I strode in and Ella was working the counter, sweat dripping down her dark face. We waited in line and when it was our turn I had to ask Ella, "Why are you so busy today? It can't be from the book signing at Diversions Tea House, surely?"

Ella eyed the manager who stood nearby and replied, "No, but can I get your order? I don't have much time to talk today."

"We'll each have a two piece meal with mashed potatoes."

"And a diet soda," El added with a nod. "We're trying to cut back."

"If that's the case, you sure wouldn't be eating here," Ella said with a wink. After I paid and we had our meals, I said, "I'd sure love your take on why this place is so packed."

"It's the Bigfoot thing. It hit the news today that they're planning to film a reality show here, so plenty of gawkers have come to town in hopes of getting an audition."

"They're doing auditions? I thought they just planned to find proof that Bigfoot really is roaming the woods."

"From the sound of it—"

"A line is forming," the manager bellowed with a reddened face.

Ella's neck snapped around and she glared at him. "I ain't no slave, you know." Gasps were heard all around. Since Ella was African American, it hit home like a sledgehammer. "I deserve a break." With that she strutted away, joining us in the lobby. El and I carried our trays over to a table and sat down, huddling together as we spoke.

"So, Ella. Why are they doing auditions?"

"Well, what I heard was they want to form teams and will be looking for Bigfoot with a prize of ten million dollars."

"I've heard about the money. Perhaps that's why Billy Matlin hired us."

"He hired you to do what?"

"Find Bigfoot on his property."

"He's using you to claim the prize money all for himself?"

"I'm not sure, but I sure would like to find out."

"We should head out to his place after lunch," El suggested.

"We will—right after we question Elsie Bradford. Plus, I sure don't want to miss all those cats clambering all over her property," I said with a glint in my eye. "And maybe take a few pictures for a keepsake."

"Or possibly post on Facebook," El suggested.

"That won't do. She might be on Facebook."

"She is," Ella said. "There're a bunch of us older ladies who meet in a private location to do just that. There are even a few kids who are helping us learn how to be computer literate."

Eleanor rubbed her hands together. "Oh, how fun. You mean like an after-hours bar?"

"Sort of," she smiled. "Of course, there's always a designated driver since Elsie makes up a batch of her spiked lemonade."

"I'd love to go sometime," Eleanor said.

"Aww, I'm not supposed to tell anyone, and it's a private group. Elsie is very particular about who is allowed in."

I cocked a brow. "Oh, really? We'll keep your secret, won't we, El?" I said as I nudged her in the ribs.

"Yup, mum's the word."

Instead of telling us what we wanted to know, Ella went back to work. We finished our food, and it wasn't until we were back in the car and heading toward Elsie's that El spit out, "Of all the nerve. I thought we were Elsie's friends, too."

"We are, but you know how she can be. She's the queen bee of the Tawas area social circles. We probably intimidate her since we're investigators and all."

"If it weren't for us, Elsie wouldn't—"

"Stop it right now, El. We can't talk about the past now. We have a case to keep on track."

"Hunting Bigfoot? This is the lamest case *ever*, if you ask me."

"At least we haven't found any corpses. Be happy with that."

"Not yet, anyway, but I don't see how you can be so darn happy with this case when there is no such thing as Bigfoot."

"You sure were a believer when you thought you saw something in the woods behind Billy's place that first day."

"Well," Eleanor frowned in hesitation, "I'm a little worried about all this hoopla. What if someone thinks we're nuts and locks us away?"

"From the sounds of it, we're not the only ones thinking Bigfoot might be real. Plus, it takes way more than that before they lock you up. I think they need a court hearing at the very least."

"I suppose. This is just not a case that I imagined we'd ever get involved in."

I would have reminded her about our other cases, but kept my lips zipped as Elsie's house came into view. As I rolled up the drive, I saw that indeed Elsie had taken on the responsibility of taking care of the Cat Lady's felines, like twenty of them from the looks of the yard. There were yellow cats sauntering across the lawn, black and white ones lounging on the porch, and white ones peeking out beneath the hedges.

"They certainly look tamer than they did at Bernice's house. I wonder what Elsie's secret is?"

I had no idea, but I certainly hoped that we could get to the door without being bombarded by the felines. I cut the engine and El and I crept outside, making way for the door. I swallowed hard when the cats eyed us up, but thus far they remained where they were. I really had to get Elsie's secret.

I knocked at the door and Elsie appeared in her usual powder blue ensemble. Her hair was bleached blonde, but her baby blues softened as she said, "Hello, girls. Come inside."

As we walked through the door, her latest dog, Zeus, a pit bull with gray striped fur, greeted us. I gulped, but Elsie assured us, "Don't worry about him. He's as gentle as a lamb, but he sure doesn't like cats much. I suppose it was a mistake allowing the Cat Lady to convince me that I should keep her cats here for a while, but she promised me a share of the prize money when she finds Bigfoot."

I squared my shoulders. "So you actually believe in Bigfoot, then?"

"I've sure seen something near here. I can't say if it's Bigfoot or not, but whatever it is, it's big."

"So you're saying you saw Bigfoot?"

"No, I just said I saw something big, brown and hairy."

"What road?"

"Well, not but half a mile from here. As you know, Cat Lady doesn't live far from here, and neither does Billy Matlin, who started this whole thing. If only he hadn't blabbed about what he'd seen. But I suppose it's of no matter now that the cat is outta the bag, so to speak. All we can do now is figure out if what he saw is the same thing many of us have seen in the area."

"I see. Well, aren't you concerned that someone might think you're nuts? I imagine that's what most folks in town think of Billy Matlin."

"Oh, is that what you think then? That Billy is nuts?"

"I can't say for certain. All I know is that there is something strange going on here. El and I just have to figure out what."

"What do you think, Eleanor? I can imagine you have your own opinions."

Eleanor sighed. "I think so much better when I'm not so parched. Do you have any of your specialty lemonade handy?"

Elsie smiled and glided into the other room, returning with a pitcher of lemonade and three glasses. "As a rule, I never drink before six, but I'd hate for you girls to not have a glass of my lemonade. It's been awhile since I've seen you girls." She poured the lemonade and continued, "I heard you took on Billy's case. So you must realize that there is something worthwhile to investigate."

"We're not sure just yet, but the U.S. Fish and Wildlife Service is investigating."

"Oh, really? So they must think there is some merit to the case?"

"Yes," El said. "It seems Bigfoot might be responsible for killing bald eagles since the remains of one was found on Billy's property."

"Like El said, the fish and game people take the killing of an endangered animal seriously, even though the bald eagle isn't endangered anymore."

"It's still protected, "El said. "Hopefully they can find evidence that will support the fact that Bigfoot is indeed in Tawas, but more importantly, Cat Lady needs to find solid evidence for the prize money. That's the reason I took in her cats like I have."

I decided to keep to myself the fact that Bernice won't be getting a share of the prize money even if Bigfoot was found. I wasn't about to open that can of worms. "I figured as much, but I'm actually surprised you did that. I've never known you to take a liking to cats."

"Not at all. I'm even a little allergic, if you need to know."

"Elsie, I don't see any oxygen tubing. Aren't you still on oxygen?"

"Not anymore. Doctor Thomas told me I'm doing fine without it with my recent test, but it's sure a hassle when I have to feed the varmints outside. Lucky for me, they run off when Zeus goes outside."

"Is Cat Lady recouping your losses, or paying for the food at least?"

"Not hardly, but she'll make it good once she finds Bigfoot."

"What makes you think we won't find Bigfoot first?" El asked.

"That's highly doubtful. Bernice has a whole film crew at her house. All you girls have is crazy Billy Matlin telling you stories."

"Why is Billy any more crazy than everyone else who claims to have seen Bigfoot?" I asked, aggravated.

"No sense in getting in an uproar about this, Aggie. I just think those guys from the Animal Network know what they're doing is all."

"Hogwash," El spat. "I bet all they plan to do on that Hunting Bigfoot show is tromp around in the woods."

Elsie raised a brow as we downed our spiked lemonade. "Calm down, now. This isn't a competition between us, but my money is on the Cat Lady."

"Bernice is fruitier than a peck of apples," El said with a nod of her head. "And you know it, Elsie."

"We'll see, but until then, no sense in ruffling your feathers over it. Of course, if you want to take part in the hunt, why not audition for the show? It might help you get some inside knowledge."

I shook my head. "You expect us to tromp out in the woods with the rest of the yokels?"

"Why not? It's not like you haven't done that before."

I had to agree with that one, but I couldn't imagine either El or I would stand a chance of getting selected for the reality series, but what the hay. I was game. We thanked Elsie and left. I wanted to head back to Billy's and ask him a few more questions, like did he really hire us to find Bigfoot so that he could win the ten million dollar prize?

When Eleanor yawned, I knew that we'd have to save the interrogating for another day. Elsie's spiked lemonade had done its magic and I felt as bushed as Eleanor looked. I rolled into Eleanor's driveway and followed her inside the house. While Eleanor retired to her bedroom for a nap, I conked out on the sofa, listening to the waves that lapped the shore of Lake Huron. It was so soothing. All I had at home was the sound of crickets chirping that nowhere near lulled me to sleep. It didn't take long before I fell asleep with visions of Bigfoot in my dreams.

Chapter Nine

Waves pummeled the beach as they crashed to shore. Outside the sky was cloudy and overcast—a storm was undoubtedly brewing. Strange, since the last I had heard it wasn't supposed to rain until tomorrow. I swung my legs off the edge of the sofa and stood, rubbing the soreness from my nagging hip. Is it possible that El and I had fallen asleep for the rest of the night, and that it was indeed morning?

I knocked on El's bedroom door and she called out for me to come in. Eleanor was sitting on the bed, plucking her eyebrows in front of a 10x magnified mirror. "What time is it?" I asked.

With tweezers poised to pluck another eyebrow hair, El said, "Eight in the morning. I guess I was so exhausted that I slept half the day away and all night. How long have you been awake, Aggie?"

"Actually, I just woke up myself. I haven't slept like that in some months. I guess I was exhausted, too."

"Probably for the best since we need to try out for that hunting Bigfoot show. Do you think we stand a chance at winning a spot?"

"Not likely, but it's worth a shot. I'd rather stop by Billy's place beforehand, though. Just to find out if he's using us to claim the prize money."

"Do you really think he'll tell us the truth even if we do ask?"

"There's only one way to find out," I said as I left the room, intent on brewing a pot of fresh coffee. Eleanor didn't make it into the kitchen until I had poured a cup of the strong brew.

Eleanor was dressed in denim pants with a white tee shirt. In her hand was a pair of pink crop pants with a matching pink button up shirt. "I meant to give this to you earlier, but now is the right time since I can't allow you to be traipsing around town in the same clothing you wore yesterday. What would the locals say?"

"I'm not sure they even knew what I wore yesterday, but I appreciate the fresh clothes." I went in the bathroom and changed, splashing cool water on my face. When I walked into the kitchen again, El had a cup of coffee that smelled of French vanilla creamer, just the way I liked it.

"We'd better get a move on and catch Billy before he has a chance to slip off somewhere. I wonder if he's really competing with that Brent guy from the Animal Network," El said.

"I wonder who is really putting up the prize money."

"Beats me, Aggie, but we aren't gonna find out hanging around here all day." She walked to the door and I cut off the coffee machine and grabbed my purse, following Eleanor out the door.

I turned onto US 23 and couldn't help but notice all the traffic heading toward East Tawas. "I bet all those cars are people wanting to audition for that Bigfoot show."

"I bet you're right, Aggie. Hopefully, Billy can shed more light on what is really going on around the Tawas area."

"I sure hope so."

Ten minutes later I made the turn into Billy's house. I was glad that his truck was in the drive, at least. The sooner he answered our questions, the sooner El and I could prepare for auditioning for that reality show. When El and I made our way toward the house, I couldn't help but notice how deadly silent it was. Not one bird singing, not a cricket chirping, nothing. I felt like we were in a dead zone. An involuntary shudder began that I was unable to control. Was I worried what Billy might say, or—"

"Look, Aggie. The door is ajar," El observed.

I was a bundle of nerves by now, for sure. I pulled out my cell phone and called 911, reporting suspicious activity out at the Matlin place.

When I hung up, Eleanor said, "Wasn't that a bit premature?"

"No, there is definitely something amiss here."

"Should we wait until the cops show up then?"

"Not at all. We'll just be sure not to touch anything." I pushed the door open with my knee and I couldn't believe what I saw. Billy's house was completely trashed. Sofas and tables were overturned, but what startled me the most was that the patio door was shattered and covered with a red substance on the outside that appeared to be blood.

I exchanged a wide-eyed glance with Eleanor who gulped hard. "Maybe we should really wait outside for the cops to show up?"

"Not just yet. We should take a look around just in case Billy is hiding somewhere."

"I've never seen a patio door shattered like that. You can tell that the glass was broken from the outside."

Sure enough it was easy to see that she was dead-on right since most of the glass shards were inside, not outside. I carefully walked down a long hallway, sneaking a peek inside a bedroom, but it looked normal. The bed wasn't disturbed and the beige comforter was in place. I picked up a sock from atop the dresser and opened the closet, moving the hangers aside to determine if Billy was hiding in there somewhere, but it was empty.

Eleanor was standing in the hallway, waiting on me. "The bathroom's empty," she announced.

"Same for the bedroom," I said as I made my way back into the living room. I entered the kitchen next where a teapot was lying on the floor discarded, but everything else looked exactly like it should. The sink was spotless, dishes piled in the drain rack. All of the cupboards were closed, too. I opened what I thought might be a closet, but it was a pantry, and empty save for shelves filled with canned and boxed food.

El and I went into the living room just as Sheriff Peterson and Trooper Sales walked in with their guns drawn. El and I raised our hands and I said, "It's clear in here. We already took a look see around."

"Why are you even here?" Peterson asked.

"Well, Billy Matlin hired us to find, you know ... Bigfoot, and we came to ask him a few questions, but found the front door ajar."

"Aggie thought it was a good idea to check it out."

"Not the smartest move," Trooper Sales said as he holstered his revolver. "You both could have put yourselves in grave danger."

"I called 911 and reported that there was something amiss here at least."

"Still," Sheriff Peterson said. "It would be safer for you two to wait on us to check things out."

I pointed out the glass. "It appears that the window was broken from the outside in, like they wanted something in here."

"Something like Bigfoot," El added. "We searched all the rooms, but we couldn't find Billy anywhere."

"Exactly. There is a teapot on the floor in the kitchen. I think Billy must have dropped it when he heard the window break."

"Yes," El cut in. "When he came out here to check things out, that's when it got him."

"When *what* got him?" Sheriff Peterson asked.

"Bigfoot, of course," El said.

Sheriff Peterson and Trooper Sales exchanged a look with widened eyes. "I see," Sales said. "How did you gather that?"

"From the blood outside, of course," I said. "Bigfoot must have dragged him outside, and that's probably when Billy was injured."

"Bigfoot might have eaten him," El said. "But that's weird since Billy has been feeding him all along."

I nodded in agreement. "Perhaps he forgot to feed him today, El."

El clapped her hands. "That must be it, but is Bigfoot a carnivore?"

"I fancy him more of an omnivore, El."

"A what?"

"You know, an animal that eats both meat and plants, or humanoid, since we really don't know what Bigfoot is for sure, man or animal."

"A very hairy man."

"Are you two done yet?" Sales asked. "I wonder if we'll ever figure out what really happened, since the two of you have invaded the crime scene, and probably destroyed any evidence we would have gathered."

"Would have? Don't you mean you intend to gather?" I showed them my sock-covered hand. "I was careful not to leave any fingerprints on anything."

Sheriff Peterson unsuccessfully stifled a chuckle. "Great idea, but perhaps you two should wait outside while we investigate the scene."

Before either El or I had the chance to say anything, Sales asked. "Why were you two here?"

"I already told you. Billy hired us to find Bigfoot, but we were given some information and we wanted to ask Billy a few questions."

Sales smoothed his hair back with a hand. "Such as?"

"Just that we heard there is prize money at stake for finding Bigfoot to the tune of ten million."

That got their attention. "I see," Sheriff Peterson said. "Well, who is putting up that kind of money?"

"Heck if I know. All I do know is that the Animal Network plans to shoot a reality show soon. It's called Hunting Bigfoot."

El tapped her foot. "They're shooting it at—"

I tapped El's toe just enough to silence her as I added; "They're shooting near here. I forget where."

"That's all we need in East Tawas," Sheriff Peterson began. "Before long, we'll have big game hunters showing up in town. East Tawas barely survived the last hoopla spawned by the two of you."

"I don't care for how you said that, Peterson. Was it my fault that East Tawas had ghost hunters in town that one time, or treasure hunters the other? No. Folks just get riled up when something out of the ordinary happens. It's our duty to stay on this case and figure out what might have really happened to Billy Matlin."

"At this point, he's merely missing," Peterson said. "We'll gather up some hounds and see if they can get a scent after we scour the woods a bit on our own. That means without the two of you interfering. It's bad enough you have those DNR and U.S. Fish and Wildlife guys fighting over evidence gathered here."

"So you do know about that?" I asked.

"Yes, and I'm not about to allow you to do the same thing you did with them. You'll leave our crime scene and get out of our way so that we can investigate on our own."

With that, Sheriff Peterson and Trooper Sales split up and checked the house, just like we already had."

"What should we do, Aggie?"

"I don't know, but we can't allow them to shove us aside. Hurry, let's go out back and check things out before either of them realizes where we went. Perhaps they'll just think that we left, or are waiting in the car."

Eleanor and I carefully stepped over the glass, and within a few minutes, we followed the trail of the drops of blood that led into the woods. "Watch out for the stick, Eleanor," I said.

"It's sure getting harder to follow this trail. I hope we don't come across Billy's body ripped to shreds. I don't think my stomach could handle that."

I led the way on the trail that wasn't too bad, but narrowed slightly just as I heard a whopping sound. El clung to my arm. "Is that ... Bigfoot?"

Birds flew overhead and the bushes shook ahead of us. Eleanor's fingernails bit into my arm, but I gripped her arms just as tight. My heart nearly leapt out of my chest as a white-tailed deer burst from the underbrush and reared back slightly when its large brown eyes met ours, dashing on in the opposite direction.

"He sure looked spooked," Eleanor observed. "Maybe we should get out of here while the getting is good."

"I'll agree with that." El and I went back the way we came and rushed past the troopers who combed through the woods. Guns were drawn as we startled them, and Sheriff Peterson shouted, "What in tarnation are you two doing? Trying to get shot?"

"Yes," Trooper Sales added. "I recalled the sheriff telling you two to leave the crime scene. Get in your car and go home. We can handle the search."

The sound of dogs was heard as a handler came forward with two German Shepherds with bared teeth, snapping their jaw at us. Luckily for us, they were controlled enough that neither of us suffered a nasty bite. Those dogs were quite capable of tearing us limb from limb, and I knew it.

"We didn't run across Billy, but we heard an awful noise. I've never heard anything like it before."

"It was a whopping sound," Eleanor added. "My bet is that it was Bigfoot by the way a white-tailed deer came running out of the bushes. I know it was as scared as us."

"I see. Well, move along now, and leave this time," Sales said. "I'd hate to arrest the two of you just to keep you out of the crime scene."

My bet is that wouldn't go so well for him at home with my granddaughter, Sophia. "What do you think happened here, Sales?"

He scratched his arm, swatting at the mosquitos. "I'm not sure, just yet. We'll be handling it as a missing person's case until we find something that leads us to believe otherwise."

"What about that blood?"

"There's a forensics tech gathering samples. At this point we don't know if it's blood at all, or even if it is, if it belongs to Billy Matlin. Don't worry yourselves, we'll figure it out."

Chapter Ten

El and I made for our car and left, heading for town. I looked at the clock and it wasn't even noon yet. I pulled into the campground and soon Eleanor and I were waiting outside Martha's Winnebago as I rapped on the door.

She peeked out the door and opened it just enough for us to come in. Martha still wore her bathrobe, and her eyes red and puffy.

"Are you alone?" I asked.

"Of course I am. Why would you think otherwise?"

"Well, the last time we saw you, you were with Joshua Crabtree, I believe. I just thought he was ... you know—"

"Your latest boy toy," Eleanor finished for me.

"He's helping me make jewelry, that's all."

"So you're trying to tell me that you're not entertaining the young men these days?"

"Not lately. Since when do you even care, Mother?"

"Hitting a dry spell are you?" Eleanor asked, always the one to try and extract additional information.

"It's not like that exactly. It's just that ever since I became a grandma, I've re-evaluated my lifestyle is all. I don't want to be the laughing stock of East Tawas."

"I honestly never thought that mattered to you, Martha. Being a grandma doesn't mean you can't continue to live your life to the fullest."

Eleanor's brow arched sharply. "Are you suddenly condoning your daughter's activities as a cougar?"

"I've adjusted to who Martha is, and I'm fine with it."

"That sounds harsh, Mother. So is that how you see me, as a middle aged floozy?"

"What is going on, Martha? I accept you for who you are and now you're trying to tell me you're someone else. So how do you see yourself?"

"Right now, I'm someone with a hangover. I met that author, Madison Johns, for drinks, and I'm afraid I drank too much, but she kept buying them so what's a girl to do?"

"Say no," I said with a smile. I made a pot of coffee while Eleanor brought Martha up to speed regarding what had happened this morning and how Billy Matlin was presumed missing.

"So you think Bigfoot dragged Billy off into the woods?" Martha asked.

"It sure looks that way, but unless his body is found, we'll never really know what did happen."

"Sounds like quite the story. I'm not sure about these Bigfoot stories. It seems far fetched to me."

"Really, Martha?" El asked. "I expected that you'd have more of an open mind."

"And why is that?"

"No reason, really. I guess I don't know who you really are after all. It was a lot easier when you were a cougar—that I get," Eleanor said with a wink.

I waited for the dripping of the coffee pot to stop and poured each of us a cup, carrying them to the dinette benches where Martha and Eleanor sat. I then retrieved the vanilla creamer and poured enough in my cup to flavor it. When I sat down, Martha had her face over her cup, allowing the rising steam to drift into her nostrils.

"Whatever your plans are today, Mother—leave me out of them."

I leaned my back against the floral cushion of the bench. "Oh, really? So you don't want to go with El and me when we audition for that reality show, Hunting Bigfoot?"

That got Martha's attention. "You two on a reality show about Bigfoot? This I gotta see firsthand."

We finished our coffees while Martha took her shower, appearing twenty minutes later wearing camouflage pants and shirt, her wild blonde hair flowing about her shoulders.

"Wow, Martha," Eleanor said. "You sure spruced up quick."

"I can't wait to meet Brent. He sure looks cute on that Animal Network show *Hunting Bigfoot*."

I shook my head. "You mean Hunting Bigfoot. *Finding Bigfoot* is on the Animal Channel."

"So I suppose the Tawas Bigfoot isn't big enough of a deal for the Animal Channel, but I'll settle for Hunting Bigfoot. How hard do you think it will be to get selected?"

"I'm not sure, but I do know that it's being taped at the Cat Lady's house, so hopefully we can convince Brent to pick us. It's the least he can do since Bernice is allowing him on her land."

"Who?" Martha asked confused.

"The Cat Lady's real name is Bernice Riley. It's still hard for me to call her that, but perhaps I should start." I stared down at our apparel. "It might be a good idea if we wore camouflage to the audition, too, don't you think Martha?"

"I'm not sure they have any in your sizes."

Eleanor's brows drew together. "And that means what, exactly?"

"Nothing," Martha quickly countered. "I meant I don't think Walmart has any camouflage clothing this time of year."

Eleanor whisked back a stray lock of hair. "Well, Walmart isn't the only place to shop, you know. We could check out Nordic Sports. It's on West Bay Street."

"Fine," Martha said, "but don't set your hopes on finding any clothing like that. This isn't even hunting season yet."

We meandered our way out the door, and soon were off down the road, arriving at Nordic Sports within minutes. The exterior of Nordic Sports was all wood and reminded me of a cabin you might find in the woods. When we opened the door, a bell jingled overhead and we made our way inside. Shelves were filled with everything from camping and fishing, to hunting supplies—anything you'd need on an outdoor adventure.

Eleanor examined the Kayaks near one wall with interest. "I've always wanted to try this out."

I raised a brow. "Me, too, but we're much too old to be doing anything that radical."

"Speak for yourself."

"Be reasonable, Eleanor. Can you imagine us sitting in something like that? Who on earth would help us get out of the blasted thing?"

Eleanor erupted into a fit of giggles. "I guess you're right, Aggie, but it does look like fun. She strode to the counter and asked the woman behind the glass counter for help locating camouflage clothing in our size."

Instead of being judgmental, like Martha suggested she would be, the woman went into the back and presented us with what we requested. "Where are you ladies going dressed in camo?" the woman asked.

"We're auditioning for a reality show, Hunting Bigfoot."

Still without judging, she suggested proper footwear. "You sure don't want to be tromping out in the woods without boots."

Martha shook her head at the woman with the reddish curly hair. "You're quite the saleswoman, I'll give you that. Don't you think it's kinda crazy for two elderly ladies to be looking for Bigfoot?"

"Not at all. It seems like half the town has gone Bigfoot crazy. At least, ever since Billy Matlin started telling everyone his story."

"What do you make of his story?" I asked.

The woman put her hands on her hips. "Well, who am I to call the kettle black? I've seen some pretty strange things, too. Just last night my hounds sure were spooked at something and took off. I haven't seen them since."

"Do you think Bigfoot got them?" Eleanor asked.

"I'm not sure, but they've never acted like that before. I hope this gets figured out soon. I, for one, would like to know what's been going on out at the Matlin place. He's a nice enough fella. I can't imagine him just making the story up."

"Do you know him?" I asked.

"Oh, no. Nothing like that. He comes in sometimes, but he's only been asking about maps of the area."

"Maps?"

"Sure, I can show you." She disappeared behind the counter and handed us a few maps. "Trail maps for the most part."

"Thanks," I said. "Are these the same ones you gave to Billy?"

"Yes, hiking trails and ski trails. There are twelve different trails in all."

"Thanks." When I turned to Eleanor, she was examining the labels of the North Face clothing. "What on earth are you doing, Eleanor?"

"Making sure these are authentic North Face clothing. There are plenty of fakes out there."

Before I had the chance to say a word, the clerk agreed. "Yes, you're right, but ours are the real deal. We sure wouldn't have been in business this long if we cheated customers with fakes. We're an authorized dealer of these brands, and fully guarantee the products we carry."

We set out the clothing on the counter and paid for our purchases. "So, you haven't actually seen Bigfoot in the area then?"

"Nope, just heard an awful noise at night, sometimes."

"What kind of noise? What did it sound like?"

"It was sort of a whopping noise. I can't really explain it any other way."

I thanked the woman and we went back outside and into the car.

"See, Bigfoot is real," Eleanor said.

"I wish you'd make up your mind, Eleanor."

"I'm totally convinced since we were at Billy's house this morning. What else would be able to crash through his patio door?"

"A white-tailed deer," Martha said.

"I can't imagine any deer shattering a whole window like that," I countered. "I'm with El, here. There was blood, too. My bet is that Bigfoot dragged poor Billy off into the woods and possibly ate him."

"Oh, and did you find any evidence to support that theory?" Martha asked.

"Well, no, but we didn't get a chance to finish our investigation. As it was, the cops were there and didn't know we had snuck off to check out the woods."

"How exactly did you manage that, Mother? I can't imagine two old ladies could sneak around that easily."

"We could when Sheriff Peterson and Trooper Sales were checking out the house. I guess they thought we left as we were told."

"Seems like those two would know enough to personally escort you out to your car and make sure you drove off."

"I guess they were just too intent on checking out the house."

Eleanor shifted in her seat. "Lucky for us you don't work for the sheriff's department. You'd tell them all of our secrets."

"You don't have any secrets. Neither of you know how to keep your mouths closed for long."

I gripped the steering wheel hard, braking as a man with a rifle on his shoulder crossed the road. "Oh, my. I should call this in. We can't have some deranged man waltzing all over town with a firearm."

"Nope, not until hunting season at least," El said. She pulled out her cellphone and reported what she saw to the 911 operator."

When I arrived at the Cat Lady's house, it was quite packed with vehicles parked every which way. "I sure hope we get the chance to get on this reality show," I said. "I'd hate to think that we'd be excluded simply on account of our age."

"You might want to use that reasoning," Martha said. "It sure has worked for you in the past. 'Selective old age' I think they call it. On the one hand, you both seem to get mad when someone calls you old, and on the other, you act all-frail like to get your way. If I were you, I'd—"

"Oh, shut up already, Martha. I knew we should have left you at home," I said, irritated, although she did have a point.

"Don't blame me, Mother. I'm just speaking the truth."

"You could do a whole lot less speaking right now. We need to get on that show."

"Then act like able-bodied, strong senior citizens like you keep saying you both are. Hold back on the riot act about discriminating against the elderly and only use it if it's necessary."

"Good point, Martha. Sorry for telling you to shut up. I guess we rub each other the wrong way sometimes."

"Enough said. Hurry up and park before we don't get a chance to get in the door."

I parked and we walked toward the door. As we did, we saw a familiar face. A short senior-aged lady with kind green eyes came forward and Eleanor hugged her tight. As they pulled away Martha asked, "Who is this lovely lady?"

"I'm Margarita Hickey, Eleanor's sister. I live in Bear Paw."

"How nice," Martha said.

I smiled kindly, a tad nervous. I'd never met Eleanor's sister before, but she had a similar facial structure as Eleanor's. "Hello, I'm Agnes Barton."

Margarita gave me a hug. When she pulled away, her face had lit up. "I've heard so much about you. It's like we're old friends already."

That sure made me relax. "Thanks, but what are you doing in town?"

"I came with them." She pointed out a fiery redhead holding an archery bow and a blonde-haired woman with wilder hair than Martha. She then went on to explain, "The one with the bow is Tammy Rodrigue, and the blonde is Dixie Perriloux. They're from Louisiana and have been here since last winter when Tammy won the Tournament of Trouble in Bear Paw. We've become good friends and they've even helped me revamp my restaurant, Hidden Pass. I now serve Cajun food. We've even done a bit of investigating, too. Didn't Eleanor tell you?"

El shrugged. "It slipped my mind."

Did it really slip her mind, or didn't Eleanor want me to know that we're not the only ones in the state of Michigan who dabble in investigations? "So, why are you here?"

"Tammy wants to audition for the reality show."

I motioned to her bow. "You do know that it's not a big game hunt, right?"

"Of course I do, but no way am I tramping out in the woods without my baby here," Tammy said. She locked eyes with me. "So, you're Agnes Barton. I almost thought you were a myth the way Margarita went on about you and her sister. You seemed larger than life."

I smiled at what sounded almost like a compliment. "Thanks, I think."

"Why are you here? Is there a major crime wave that I can help you out with?"

I shook my head. "Nope. We're here to compete in the show, same as you. If we get picked, that is."

"Is it safe for you two to be tromping out in the woods like that? I'd hate to see legends like you get hurt."

I tried to figure out if she was kissing up to us for a reason, or just wanted to get rid of us so she'd have more of a chance. "Thanks, but we're used to the rugged life." I held up my bags. "We just need to change, is all. We have everything we need in this bag."

The door was opened and we were instructed to come inside. El and I walked in first and spotted Bernice, who offered us a place to change. When we came back out donning our camouflage clothing, more than a few snickers were heard in the room from a group of men near the corner of the room.

A man dressed in jeans and a plaid shirt introduced himself as Brent Hunter, obviously not his real name. There had to be a pun in there somewhere. "We're forming two teams. Each of you will have an opportunity to show us what you got." He walked over to Tammy and said, "You don't need a bow, sweetheart. You already have my attention."

"The last man that said that almost wound up with an arrow in his crotch," Tammy calmly stated.

"Playing cool. I like that. But seriously, there's no need to carry that with you on this hunt."

"Oh, so you'd have me believe there're no wild animals in the woods?"

"Just me," he snickered.

"That's *so* not true," Eleanor said. "There are coyotes and bears, and Bigfoot. I, for one, would feel comfortable knowing that we'd have some protection."

"Not to worry, ladies," Brent said. "I have plenty of protection." He winked suggestively at Tammy, who tightened her grip on her bow.

"Just so we're clear. I'm here to hunt Bigfoot and no other reason."

Brent moved in closer, Tammy kicked his feet out from under him, and Brent landed with a thump on the floor. "I want her on my team," Eleanor announced.

"Stop, Eleanor. She never said she'd even want us on her team."

"We sure don't want you on *our* team," a man near the patio door said with a sneer."

My hands flew to my hips. "Who'd want to be on your team anyway? Do you plan to pay off your child support debt with the prize money, Barney?"

Tammy and Dixie chuckled. "Gee, Barney. How much do you owe?" Dixie asked.

He shuffled his feet, silenced at least for now.

Brent turned to Eleanor and me. "Aren't you two kinda—?"

"It's so important for your safety not to finish that sentence, young man," I interjected.

Brent gulped. "I'm sure surrounded by a bunch of bad-assed women. What's a guy to do?"

Shut up and get on with it, was my thought. "So are we planning to start today or next week when all the big game hunters show up in town?"

"This is not a big game hunt."

"I've seen a man carrying around a rifle not half an hour ago," I said.

Brent climbed back to his feet like nothing happened. "I'll have to talk to the director if he wants to risk having one of you older gals on the show. I'm not sure if viewers would care to see that on a reality show."

"Why not? If they can have those guys from Duck Dynasty on the tube, or those swamp people, they certainly can handle a few senior citizen ladies who happen to solve crimes in their spare time."

Brent's attitude changed. "I like that angle. Like what kind of crimes … purse snatchers?"

"Nope, we've solved mostly murder cases. We're what they call 'amateur sleuths.'"

"Like Jessica Fletcher?"

I was so getting sick of the references to that *Murder, She Wrote* character. "Sort of, except that we're real and she's not."

"Of course. Sure you are."

"You could always check with Sheriff Peterson if you don't believe me," I said.

The Cat Lady entered the room. "Show my friends some respect, would you?"

"I thought I told you to stay out of sight," Brent said.

Gasps were heard and Tammy's eyes narrowed to slits. "Of all the nerve. How have you gotten this far insulting your elders? If you lived back in Louisiana, someone would have fed you to the gators by now. Show your elders some respect. They've lived through some pretty hard times, and are wise beyond their years."

Brent ran a hand through his thick brown hair. "Fine, but what do you ladies possibly know about Bigfoot?"

"I know Bigfoot smells like a dirty dog and dirty socks. I know he makes a lot of noise when he tromps through the woods," I said.

"He also makes a whooping noise," Eleanor added.

"You … how do you know that?"

"Because we've smelled and heard him in the woods. Why else do you think we're here? We're just as capable of hunting Bigfoot as any of you."

A portly man with a bald head approached us and gave us a waiver to sign. "Just in case you ladies try to sue, we're not responsible."

I examined the form and Eleanor and I signed, as did the rest of the would-be hunters. When Tammy handed back her paper, she announced, "Don't even *think* about asking me to surrender my bow."

"Not at all. I love a sexy woman with a weapon," Brent said as he walked away.

"Wow, Tammy. You're sure a standup gal. I haven't met too many women like you in my lifetime. Not at your age, anyway."

"Thanks, Agnes, but I can see I'm probably gonna have to put a hurting on that Brent before long."

"Besides the one you already did, you mean?"

"He should mind his manners. It's not healthy for a man to approach me like that."

Dixie giggled. "I didn't even get a chance to stop you this time. She can't help herself. Tammy's just not the type to stand for any bull from a man, and I can already see that Brent character isn't going to change his tune."

"Nope," I said. "He seems pretty full of himself."

Margarita was in the corner, observing us. "You girls sure know how to shake it up. I need to be more like you."

That surprised me. "You're sure not a thing like Eleanor. Are you positive you two are related?"

"We sure are and I have to admit that we're much different. I could use more of her spunk, though."

"You're spunky enough when you need to be, Margarita. It takes plenty of spunk to start dating at your age, or allow Dixie and me to remake your restaurant the way we have," Tammy said.

"You're dating, Margarita?" Eleanor said, surprised. "I'm glad I'm not the only one. I got engaged to a Mr. Wilson not long ago. I still haven't learned his first name."

Eleanor and Margarita laughed over that one.

"See, Tammy? If these ladies can find a man, you can too," Dixie said with a nod.

"The difference is that I don't *want* one."

"You're way too young to decide something like that. I'm sure you'll find a great man when you're ready. One who admires your spunky nature," I assured Tammy.

Chapter Eleven

We filed out the door and I pulled the Cat Lady, Bernice, aside. "So what gives?"

She stared at the ground. "I'm not sure what you mean, Agnes."

"I've never known you to allow anyone to belittle you like that. Where's all your spunk gone to?"

She raised her head and said, "Well, Brent told me to say out of sight. He seemed so nice when I met him, but he's turned out to be a real ass. When he showed up here today he started spouting out orders, and you can imagine how that went. I'd rather have shot him with my shotgun," she said solemnly. "I should have kept one of my tomcats here to scratch his eyes out. I sure miss my babies."

"I went to Elsie's and they seemed just fine. When we find Bigfoot, this will all be a distant memory."

"Do you think you can really find Bigfoot?"

"I'm not sure if this is the right time to find him, but I figure it might be a great time to search, or find Billy Matlin."

Her brow shot up. "Find Billy? Why?"

"I probably shouldn't say anything since nobody seems to know what happened."

"Please, Agnes. I promise I won't tell a soul. I certainly wouldn't tell that Brent anything."

"Okay, but you better not tell anyone."

Bernice did a motion of zipping her lip and throwing the key away.

"We went over to Billy's house this morning, and he's missing."

"Where do you expect he went?"

"Not sure, just yet. All I know was that his truck was there and his door was wide open."

I fell silent then until Bernice asked, "What else aren't you telling me?"

"That Billy's patio door was broken into from the outside and there's blood all over it."

"Do you think it's Billy's blood?"

"Not sure, just yet. I'm sure going to con either Sheriff Peterson or Trooper Sales to tell me if it is or not."

"No way will they tell you anything."

"I'll have to wait it out, is all."

Bernice scanned the tree line. "Do you think there really is a real Bigfoot?"

"I'm not sure, but Eleanor and I did hear some strange animal noises, like nothing I've ever heard before."

"Did you search for Billy in the woods?"

"Yes, but there wasn't a trace of him anywhere."

"So, that's why you came here?"

"Yes, it's another opportunity to search for Billy. He might just be hiding out in the woods."

"That, or parts of him are," Bernice said. "I'm glad you and Eleanor are here. I'll feel so much better now. I love that Tammy, whoever she is, too. I met her outside before you came. She sure will put that Brent in his place if he gets out of line again."

"I just hope she doesn't go too far. I'd hate for Brent to exclude her from the show."

"Not on your life will that happen. She makes for a good reality show character. Who wouldn't love a kick-butt type of girl for a change from all those airheads you see these days."

I waited outside with Bernice until a man with gray hair and amber eyes approached me. "I'm the director," he announced. "Peyton Daniels. I hope you don't mind Brent. He's a bit of an ass. I really love that you and Eleanor decided to audition for the reality show, but it will be quite demanding. Do you have any health issues that would exclude you from doing the show?"

"No." I was totally excluding my nagging hip from the equation, but it's been doing much better the last few months. "What exactly will it entail?"

"We'll be out in the woods shooting most of the day tomorrow, with one overnight. There's a hunters' camp behind the airport, and word has it that there's been some suspicious activity that might directly relate to Bigfoot."

"Is there really a ten million dollar prize offered if we find Bigfoot?"

"Yes, but the show is Hunting Bigfoot, remember? We don't need the Animal Channel suing us."

"Who's offering that prize, exactly?"

"That's classified," he said with a chuckle. "So far, nobody has found anything near being a Bigfoot, but I'm hopeful with all the reported Bigfoot sightings near here, we might just catch a lucky break."

I shook Peyton's hand and he left. "If I weren't already engaged, I'd sure be interested in him," I told Bernice.

"He's a real looker for sure, but I'm thinking he's just grayed prematurely. He doesn't have a wrinkle on his face."

"Of course, what movie director would? Most of them get facelifts these days, and Botox."

"Isn't that the poison that freezes your face?"

"I'm not sure, Bernice, but it certainly makes expressions impossible. Luckily, we live in a small town where that isn't done. I don't mind my wrinkles so much. I've earned every one of them."

Bernice made her way toward one of the tables that had been set up outside. She stared at the barbeque grill and asked, "Are you staying for lunch, or are you planning to do more investigating before tomorrow?"

"Tomorrow?"

"Yes, that's when the show starts."

"Early tomorrow morning," Brent said from behind me. "It seems like the old man loves the idea of having you old birds on the show."

"Why are you so darn smart-mouthed?" Eleanor wanted to know. "Didn't your mother teach you—?"

"Never had one of those. My mother took off when I was only two."

"Aww. Sorry to hear that. I didn't mean to judge you so harshly, but please don't take it out on us."

He rubbed his neck. "Sorry about that. I'll knock off the old crap if you get Tammy to have a drink with me."

"I don't think that sounds like the best idea," I said. "It seems like you have rubbed her the wrong way."

"I can't help myself. I love a fiery redhead."

"Well, she's one that doesn't love you back so you might want to back off a bit."

"She'll change her tune, they always do. She's just playing hard to get right now. Once we get in the woods, it will be game-on."

"Okay, but it's your funeral."

Brent walked away with an arrogant toss of his head.

"What an idiot," Eleanor said. "He's not even that good looking."

"Arrogance takes his looks down a notch in my book," I added.

"I'll see you tomorrow morning, Bernice. I think El and I should find Martha before she gets herself into trouble. She's sure been awfully quiet since we came here, which is so unusual."

When I walked back into the house, Martha was nowhere to be found, but Curt and Cutis Hill were here chatting it up with Tammy and Dixie. Their conversation carried far enough for me to hear it without making it appear as if I was eavesdropping, which was *so* what I was doing.

"So, you boys think you can outdo me with a bow?"

"No," Curt said with a snicker. "I said I can outshoot you."

"Oh, you must mean with a shotgun."

"Semi-automatic weapon, actually. Have you ever shot one?"

Dixie said, "That's not a weapon for sport. That's meant for destruction. Where on earth do you shoot that?"

Tammy smirked. "Boys and their big guns, or little pistols."

Curt adjusted himself. "My gun is—"

"Curt, show these ladies some manners. Ma would personally shoot us if we didn't show these ladies some respect. "I'm Curtis. Don't mind my brother. I'd sure like you to come over and we can have an archery competition—loser pays for dinner."

Tammy raised a brow at Dixie, who looked about ready to swallow her tongue. "Is there somewhere else we could go that is a little more public? My ma would shoot me if I just went to some man's house that I just met."

"We could set up targets out back," Peyton Daniels said. "We could do it right before we head out in the morning. It sounds like fun. I don't think I've ever seen a female shoot a bow before."

"Obviously, you're not from around here then," I joked. "Plenty of women go bow hunting in Michigan.

"I'm from Burbank, California, and believe me, there are so many conservation groups that if someone ever suggested hunting anything, you'd be ostracized. We can't even have fireworks, because they will interfere with the marine life."

"Oh, really? That's sure disappointing. We should get some fireworks for the ending of your show. Let it go off with a bang."

"Sounds like fun, but how do we get fireworks. Don't you need permits or something? I imagine anything too big is illegal."

Curt laughed. "Well, we know a guy who knows a guy, who could hook you up for a price."

"Great, give me the details later and I'll go over there and pick them up."

Curtis cocked a brow. "You can't go over there. We'd be happy to fetch them for you and bring them back here—if we're on the show, that is."

"Consider it a deal. I'm going have to figure out how to break up the teams. Would you boys rather be on the girl's team, or with the other men?"

"These girls?" Curt asked.

"Yes, and Agnes and Eleanor, too."

"Of course. They might just need some real men protecting them in the woods."

Tammy's eyelashes fluttered. "Of course, what would little ole me do without a real man protecting me?"

"Good one, Tammy," Dixie said as she slapped her on the back.

Eleanor and I excused ourselves and Curt and Curtis followed us out. Luckily, we were in the car by the time Curtis took off in his big redneck truck as he left a dust and stone trail in his wake.

"Sounds like those boys are sweet on Tammy, too," El pointed out. "They stand a better chance than that awful Brent. Do you think Tammy might really hurt Brent if he steps out of line?"

"Not sure about that. Let's just hope he acts more professional than he did today. I can tell she's not about to tolerate too much bad behavior from men."

"It sure makes me nervous about the Hill boys getting fireworks. I hope they don't get mixed up and bring munitions."

"I'm really surprised that they are interested in this show at all. I guess we might have spilled the beans on that one. They don't seem like the type to want the prize money."

"I'd hate to think what they'd use that money for. I'm sure the Michigan Militia doesn't need to get any bigger. Luckily, their camp isn't anywhere near here."

"Oh, they're not so bad. They just have gotten a bad repetition. They're the National Rifle Associations' best supporters."

"I just know they don't have a chapter in Iosco County. I totally support the right to bear arms. We should make sure we have ours for the show, just in case."

"In case what?"

"In case we actually meet Bigfoot in the woods and he makes us his next meal."

When I made it onto US 23, my cell phone rang. I answered it, swerving in the lane, as Martha's voice came into the receiver asking me why I had left her there. I made a wild U-turn and went back for her.

me why I had left her there. I made a wild U-turn and went back for her.

Martha got into the back when I arrived in a huff. "Of all the nerve. I can't believe you forgot me."

"Easy to do when I lost sight of you as soon as we arrived. Where were you, anyway?"

"In the kitchen, talking to the director. He told me I'd be a great assistant and hired me."

"Was this before or after your clothes were off, dear?"

"Geez, Mother. I swear you think I'm sixteen. What would it matter to you anyway?"

"It wouldn't I suppose, but I just thought you said earlier you were scaling back since you became a grandma."

"First off, I never said I slept with Peyton. You assumed it. I have skills enough to be an assistant. All they do is run errands really, or that's what he told me. I'm starting tomorrow."

"So a fetch and go girl, or woman, since you're over forty, dear. I hope he's paying you, at least."

Martha's mouth formed an O. "I guess we never got around to that part."

"Perhaps I should call Andrew and ask him to contact Peyton to make sure it's on the up and up. I'd hate to see you be taken unawares by a smooth talking California man."

Martha leaned forward in her seat. "He's sure dreamy though, isn't he?"

"He's okay, I suppose, but I wouldn't be trusting anyone associated with that reality show. Those people aren't like us, they have their own agendas."

"Like you don't. Signing up to be on a reality show to look for Bigfoot when you were already hired to do just that. It's kind of deceptive don't you think?"

"No, but there's no other way we'll be able to do a proper search of the woods with that show going on unless we're part of it."

"I really do hope you can figure out what really happened to

Billy Matlin. I'm sure it won't be long before his disappearance hits the airwaves."

"Well, they won't hear it from us. I imagine the cops will only release minimal details. Isn't that right, El?"

"Oh, sure. Whatever you say, Aggie."

"What's up with you, suddenly?"

"Oh, nothing. It just bothers me that Brent's mom left like she did. I wonder if my son acts like that since I'm out of his life."

"For one thing, you never left him. He up and decided to leave, didn't he?"

Eleanor sighed. "Not exactly. I left him with my mother so much after my divorce that I think he held it against me when he grew up."

"Didn't you just do that on account of work?"

"Not exactly. I had my men friends and they didn't much care for a woman with a child. I must admit I did neglect him and wish I could take it all back now. I really miss my boy."

"How long have you been estranged?" Martha asked.

"He never did have much to do with me, but after he put me in the County Medical Center, I told him I never wanted to see him again."

Martha rubbed Eleanor's shoulder. "Who could blame you? What an awful thing for him to do to you. How on earth did you ever get out?"

"Agnes helped me prove I still had my wits about me. It involved court hearings, but luckily the court ruled in my favor."

"I'm sure it's not your fault, Eleanor. Perhaps one day you'll be able to make amends."

"I don't really want to," Eleanor said. "But I'm still sad about him being gone. I'm just feeling a little nostalgic right now, I guess."

"It was hard for me when I went years without speaking with my mother. It took everything in me to come to East Tawas, and I must admit that I really had nowhere else to go at the time. I know that sounds bad."

I nodded. "I sure felt very put out when you did. I just didn't understand that your divorce caused you to go off the radar so much. When I couldn't get ahold of you, I just figured you didn't care about my feelings, or your daughter Sophia's, either."

"Coming home was the best decision I have ever made. I'm just happy that I've gotten the chance to reconnect with both Sophia and you. I'd hate to have missed my sweet grandbaby, Andrea. She's so precious."

"We'll all get a chance to see her today, because we're going over there. Perhaps I can pick her brain about the Matlin case."

"So you're expecting that Trooper Sales relays information to her about his job? I can't imagine that. He might still be at the Matlin place since it's just past noon now."

"He might have checked in."

"I'm all for seeing my grandbaby, but I don't think we'll get any details out of Sophia."

I drove the rest of the way to Trooper Sales house. I wasn't the happiest when he had started dating Sophia, but they seem like the ideal couple. She's a nurse at the local hospital, and he's a straight shooter Michigan State Trooper, not much different than my late husband, Tom. It took years to get over his loss, but how was I to know that I'd meet up with my former boss, Andrew Hart, at the age of seventy-two, or that we'd start dating. We're engaged now, with no wedding date in sight, but that's fine with me for now. I must say, I sure wondered when he'd come back to town. It is always so hard when he's out of town all the way in Detroit, but I rather admired his work ethics.

Chapter Twelve

I rapped on Sophia's door, and when she opened it with a grimace, I knew she was not having a great day. From the stain on her blue shirt, it was obvious the baby had spit up on her, and her usually well-kept appearance looked everything but that. She proceeded to clear the couch that had newspapers, receiving blanket, and baby toys on it. The coffee table was now piled up with the items.

She swiped a trembling hand through her hair. "Andrea has been sick all day. I finally got her to sleep."

"Sick how, throwing up?"

"Yes. I finally got her fever down, at least, but if she's not better by tonight I'm running her to the hospital."

"How awful," Martha said. "Not to worry, I'm staying with you now to help you out. Why don't you take a shower or nap and I'll take care of everything."

"Did you hear from Bill today?" I asked. "Does he know the baby's sick?"

"He's on a crime scene. He told me Billy Matlin has disappeared, and they're still conducting a search. I guess that puts a damper on your case now, Grams."

"We'll see. We're going to be on that reality show *Hunting Bigfoot* on the Animal Network."

"That's nice. Hopefully you'll be the ones to find Bigfoot. I'd love to see you show up all those men that I usually see on that show. If you'll excuse me, I'm going to crawl into bed for a few hours before Bill comes home. I'll give you a call if I end up taking Andrea in." Sophia then made her way to the back bedroom.

My heart just ached for Sophia. I glanced around at the mess in the room, and announced, "What are we waiting for? We need to clean this place up."

Martha, El, and I sorted the trash from the salvageable and the living room looked much cleaner. "We can't risk waking Sophia or the baby so vacuuming is out, but we should take a peek and see what condition the kitchen is in."

The sink was loaded with dishes. Eleanor went right to work running the dishwater and she washed while I dried and put everything away. Martha wiped off the counters and table, admiring our handiwork until an exhausted and frantic Trooper Sales came into the room. "Where's Sophia?"

"Taking a nap. The baby has been sick all day."

"I know. She called, but I was too busy at the time to talk. I should check on Andrea." He hurried from the room and came back into the kitchen, cradling the baby in his arms. "She looks hot." Sure enough, her tiny cheeks were quite pink and her breathing was a little uneven. "Grab me the thermometer, it's in the bathroom."

I did just that. We all watched as Bill took her temperature and announced, "I'm taking the baby to the hospital."

I woke Sophia up and watched helplessly as they went out the door, tearing out of the drive. I heard a jiggle and realized that Bill had left his police radio home. "The dogs lost their trail at the river, so we're wrapping up at the Matlin place. Over."

"Well, I guess that explains it then. Billy is truly missing and we need to figure out if Bigfoot is responsible or someone else," I said.

"I wonder if he has any enemies," El said. "I don't know enough about the man to say for sure."

"We could stop by Rosa Lee Hill's potpourri shop and ask her. She seems to know what's going on in town even though she keeps to herself most of the time."

"Don't forget that she used to sell medicinal Mary Jane, and who knows for sure what she sells out at her store?"

"Go ahead. I should stay here," Martha said as she wrung her hands. "I might be needed here."

"You might be of more use at the hospital, but I doubt they'd let you back to wait for the doctor with Sophia and Bill. Why not let us drop you at home? I'm sure Sophia will call you when she has news."

"You're right, but drop me off at the hospital all the same. I'd feel better if I was there—for support if no other reason."

We locked up and I was tempted to take Bill's radio, but stopped myself. I can imagine having the radio in my possession would be breaking some kind of law, for sure. Those state boys don't mess around, and I'd hate to put Bill into an awkward position with his job. He's one of my favorite troopers.

I made my way back to US 23, but after I dropped Martha off at the hospital, I made the turn going south and the traffic was bumper to bumper heading into town. My eyes widened at the shotguns I saw in the hands of passengers. "Wow, we'd better get over to the sheriff's department and give the sheriff a heads-up. It looks like big game hunters are here now."

I whirled into the parking lot and El and I rushed toward the door just as Sheriff Peterson was coming out with the DNR and U.S. Fish and Wildlife Service. "Oh, Peterson. Did you know the town is packed full of big game hunters?"

Peterson adjusted the waistband of his brown trousers. "Are you sure?"

"Well, I saw more than one car load of gun toting game hunters, or at least I think that's why they're here. I just can't believe this is happening in our town."

"It would seem that Billy Matlin's tall tales have taken on a life all their own. I'm sure it didn't help that those reality show guys decided to shoot here. I've half a mind to chase them out of town, but unfortunately, my hands are tied.

"Looks like it's about time the Department of Natural Resources gets involved," Derek said. "Come on, Patrick, we better get a move on."

"Not without me, you're not," Duane said. "The United States

Fish and Wildlife Service also have an interest here in protecting wildlife."

"Fight about it on the way then," Eleanor said. "Someone better get a handle on the situation before those folks start blasting up the woods."

Sheriff Peterson stood there with his legs shoulder-width apart. "Is that all, or do you have some other business to discuss with me?"

"Did the DNR or Wildlife Service test the hair samples from the Matlin place?"

He shook his head. "I should have known, and no to that question. They're still fighting amongst themselves. I hope that's all because I need to police the situation before it gets more out of hand."

"Nope, I guess not. Hopefully, you won't need Trooper Sales since he had to run my grandbaby to the hospital."

His brow shot up. "Nothing serious, I hope?"

"Seems the baby is sick and running a fever."

"Thanks for the update. I'll be sure not to disturb him, then. As you probably deducted by now, it's too early to determine if the blood found out at the Matlin place is really Billy's, and we still haven't found him, if you're curious."

"Thanks for the share. We're going to be on the *Hunting Bigfoot* reality show, so we'll be on the lookout for him in the woods. From the sounds of it we'll be going to that hunting camp behind the airport."

"Well, be careful out there. I'd hate to have to start a search party way out there for you. Perhaps all the people heading into town simply want to audition for the show."

We followed Peterson to his cruiser. "I sure hope you're right, Sheriff, but please be careful. East Tawas would be lost without you."

Peterson's face softened a bit. "Thanks, I think." He hopped into his car and off he went like a shot into the night.

"What did you tell him that for?" Eleanor asked.

"Well, he did tell us that they never found Billy."

"Yeah, but we already knew that."

"Yes, but we can't let him know that. We oughta try a little sugar now and then."

"I suppose so. So are we planning to question Rosa Lee Hill this year or next?"

I pulled out my cell phone and phoned in a takeout order. Ten minutes later we were waiting inside G's Pizzeria and Deli. I breathed in deeply the fragrance of garlic and tomato sauce. This place had the best pizza I've ever had in my life. My mouth was salivating already.

"I'm starving," Eleanor said. "I missed breakfast and you rushed me out of the Cat Lady's house just as she was about to grill up lunch."

"It's a good thing, too, since my grandbaby was sick. At least we were able to clean up the place for Sophia before she had to leave. I remember all too well those days when my children were sick."

Our pizza was put on the counter and the server rung us up. I handed her a twenty, telling her to keep the change and off we went. Eleanor and I got back into the car and I reminded her not to open the pizza box. "But I'm starving," Eleanor whined.

"Me, too, but we're going to give Rosa Lee a treat, and I don't want it to get cold from you opening that box."

"I sure hope she has some soda. I'm thirsty."

I drove up to Rosa Lee's potpourri shop in Tadium, right outside of East Tawas. I stared at the wooded siding. It sure hadn't changed since the days when this place was a Roy's Bait and Tackle, and when I walked in I half expected it to smell like fish, but the aroma of potpourri wafted in the air and about knocked me over. My sinus passages began to seep and I dabbed at my nose with the back of my arm.

Rosa Lee Hill came from the back wearing a black apron tied snugly around her waist, a sprig of rosemary in her weathered hands. Her eyes lit up, "Is that G's pizza I smell?"

"Sure is," I said, blinking repeatedly.

"Come on into the back. The fragrances aren't so bad back here."

We followed Rosa Lee into the back and I sunk into a chair. Once the door was closed, it wasn't so bad and felt safe enough to take a breath. "Thank goodness. I was about ready to pass out, out there."

Eleanor opened the pizza box and we each grabbed a piece of the pepperoni pizza. When I bit down, I felt like I was in heaven, or as close as I've come to it on earth.

Between bites, Rosa Lee asked, "What brings you by?"

"We've been hired by Billy Matlin to find Bigfoot." I waited for a response, but when there was none, I continued. "Anyway, he's gone missing now. His patio door was smashed in, too."

"Oh, my. Maybe Bigfoot got him," Rosa snickered. "If you believe in that nonsense, that is."

"It seems your boys, Curt and Curtis, believe it, too. They showed us a cast they took of a footprint."

"You know how boys are. They're just having a little fun with you, is all."

"Okay, so if it wasn't Bigfoot, what do you think it was?"

She stroked her chin in thought. "Not sure what you're asking here."

"Do you know anyone who'd wish to harm Billy Matlin?"

"If I were one for conspiracy theories, I'd have believed that someone wanted to shut him up."

That made perfect sense. "I see. Anyone is particular?"

"Well, folks sure got stirred up with his wild tales. He had planned to do a big interview with the Animal Channel people, but since the Animal Network is here, I just wonder if they'd rather he never did that interview. After all, they're here to do their own show. I can only imagine that the Animal Channel has way more credibility than the Animal Network, don't you think?"

"Sure, I suppose, since they have their own channel and the Animal Network is struggling, but I met some of those guys, and the director, Peyton Daniels, seems real nice. Not so much for that Brent character that's the host for the show."

"How do you know so much about that show, Agnes, if you don't mind me asking?"

"We're going to be on the show, *Hunting Bigfoot*, is why," Eleanor said. "It was all my idea, but Agnes decided it was such a great idea that she had to go along for the ride."

I raised a brow. "I did? Oh, yeah, I did. That Eleanor sure comes up with great ideas. Since Billy is missing, hopefully we'll run into him out in the woods. Any other ideas on who might have wanted Billy out of the way?"

"He has an ex-wife in town. Peggy Matlin. She works at Neiman's Market. They've had some dispute over money he owes for back child support. Besides Peggy, I can't think of anyone who'd mean him harm. He's sorta odd, but not the type to rile up too many people. From what my boys say, he sticks pretty close to home most of the time, or is out in the woods searching for Bigfoot."

"Your boys never had any squirmishes with Billy that you know of?"

Rosa Lee's hands went to her hips. "I hope you're not expecting me to know about everything my boys do. There isn't enough time in the day for that."

I wanted to ask her about her sons' activities with the Michigan Militia, and if it might have led to Billy's disappearance, but I could just as well ask Curt and Curtis outright.

El and I grabbed one more slice of pizza, opting to go out the back door to avoid the fragrances of the shop. I had a touch of asthma as a child, but I grew out of it. That is unless I'm around too many fragrances, like a flower shop or a potpourri shop.

Once we were back in the car, Eleanor and I finished our pizza and I cranked over the engine, heading back to East Tawas and Neiman's Market.

"Do you really think Billy's ex-wife had anything to do with his disappearance?" Eleanor asked.

"I'm not sure, but we need to follow the leads we're given, like it or not."

"I suppose. I'm buying a soda when we get there is all I know. I'm thirsty."

Chapter Thirteen

When we rolled into the Neiman's parking lot, it was quite busy. Not a surprise since they had the best sales in town. They had all kinds of events, from a 'Paczki' eating contest during Fat Tuesday, to the 'Taste of the Tropics' during the winter months with smoothie recipes and demonstrations. Their staff was always friendly and helpful.

We walked inside and Eleanor grabbed a soda from an ice chest and began to guzzle it, ignoring the startled expression of a woman who walked by. The folks that worked here paid it no mind since this was a common occurrence with Eleanor. They knew she'd pay on her way out.

We approached the service counter and we were waited on quickly. "Can I help you?" a woman with a cropped hairdo asked us.

"Is Peggy Matlin working today?" I asked.

"She's on break right now. Is it important?"

"Very important."

The woman led us outside where Peggy, a rotund blonde, was smoking a cigarette. I greeted her. "Are you Peggy Matlin?"

"Yes, but like I told the sheriff, I have no idea where Billy is. We're divorced."

"Oh, and what makes you think we're here to question you about your ex-husband?"

She rolled her eyes. "Because you're the private investigator, Agnes Barton, and Billy told me all about how he hired you to find Bigfoot."

"Which means what, exactly?" Eleanor asked with a tilt of her head.

"That you're here to ask me questions about Billy's disappearance. I'm sure by now word has gotten to you that he's missing. Most likely from that Trooper Sales since he's married to your granddaughter, Sophia."

I didn't like where she was going with this. "For one thing, neither Trooper Sales nor Sheriff Peterson has given us any information about Billy's disappearance. We were the ones who called them in when the house was in total disarray."

Her brow shot up. "Oh, really? Do tell."

"I'd rather not. Besides, as you said, you're divorced."

"It's not that I don't care about the man. I just can't live with him."

"I see. Is it true there was a dispute over child support money he owed?"

She bit her pinkie. "Yes, but I swear I wouldn't ever do anything to Billy except maybe lambast him with a brick."

Eleanor laughed. "Why is that?"

"Well, we were doing just fine, and then one day out of the blue he insisted that he saw Bigfoot, and that was it. All he ever did was look in the woods all day long. I tolerated it way longer than most women would, but one day I just decided that I couldn't take it anymore. I packed up my things, and me and the kids left."

"Just like that?" Eleanor asked. "Didn't you at least try to reason with him?"

"I sure did, but he just couldn't see past his Bigfoot delusions."

I straightened my shirt. "I see. So you never actually saw Bigfoot yourself?"

"No. I must admit I smelled something bad out in the backyard, but it was sewage, is all. I told him to get our septic tank drained too many times to count."

"So that's what you made of that smell?" I asked.

"Sure, what else could it be?"

"I've smelled plenty of sewage in my life, but I've never smelled anything like I did that day at Billy's place."

"I hope you aren't deluded into thinking his stories have merit. He hasn't been right since the Gulf War."

"He was in the Gulf War? Did you at least try to get him some help?"

"Yes, and he refused. I'm sorry to hear Billy disappeared, but I'm not the one to blame."

I gave Peggy a once over. She wasn't crying or even all that upset. "Are you dating anyone now?"

She bit her lip and fluffed her blonde hair a tad. "I'm not sure what you mean."

"Have you hooked up with anyone since you and Billy split? It's a simple question," Eleanor said.

"Y-Yes, but I'm sure he didn't have anything to do with Billy's disappearance."

My brow arched. "And what makes you so sure?"

"Because Bubba wouldn't do that. He's a real gentle soul, like a teddy bear."

I pressed. "Where would we find this Bubba?"

"He works at Randy's towing, but please don't go there asking questions. He hasn't been working there long. I'd hate to see him lose his job."

"What do you suggest then, because we need to ask him a few questions?"

She shrugged. "You can figure it out since you're the big time investigator, not me."

Instead of giving Peggy a piece of my mind over her last comment, I simply thanked her and made way to the cash register, waiting for Eleanor to pay for her cola.

As we walked back to the car, I mused aloud. "I suppose we could call Randy's Towing and call a wrecker, requesting Bubba to be sent out."

"What makes you think this Bubba would even be sent out to the same location his girlfriend works?"

"Good point. Let's find another spot in town to call from."

We hopped in the car and tooled down to Newman Street where I parallel parked with a thump as I ran over the curb for good measure like I always managed to do.

Eleanor laughed. "Good job. Maybe I should drive next time."

"If you did that, the car would be parked in Diversions Tea House."

Her mouth slacked open. "That's not fair. I managed to drive without incident the last two times I drove to Walmart."

"Did you, now? And how did you manage that? I thought the Caddy wasn't running?"

"I simply lifted the hood and reattached the battery cable. I'm not a dummy, you know. I know you removed it to keep me from driving."

"Fine, you can drive when we leave here, and we'll see just how well you do." I popped the hood, and took my wrench, clamoring out, and asked a kind man who strolled by to lift the hood for me, which he did.

"You want me take a look under your hood?" the man asked.

Eleanor appeared on the sidewalk and snickered. "I'd love that, but since I'm engaged it's out of the question."

"I meant look at the car engine," he said with a wink.

"Oh, drat. Thanks, but as you can see, Agnes has a wrench and can handle it. You think older gals like us can't figure out how to keep our car running?"

He held up his hands and backed away. "Not at all. Good luck, ladies." He turned on his heels and walked up the street.

I removed the cables with Eleanor playing lookout. I'd hate for anyone else to stop and ask if we needed help. Then there would be questions that I'd rather not answer. I called Randy's towing, asking for Bubba to come specifically. Instead of the dispatch woman asking questions, she told us she'd send him our way.

We strode into Diversions Tea House and we ordered a chai tea latte while we waited for the wrecker. It wasn't all that busy inside and most of the round tables were crowded with kids, each with a bubble tea, a popular item here. The bubbles were concentrated fruit juices that were dropped in the bottom of a cup that was topped off with tea. Basically the manager, Jeff, was a bartender for twelve-year-olds.

We left the tea house just as a wrecker parked alongside our car. A big-bellied man with a full beard and long hair climbed out of the wrecker and met us at the car. "What seems to be the trouble, ladies?" he asked.

"Are you Bubba?"

"Sure am. Bubba Billings, at your disposal." His big belly shook as he laughed.

"Great. So you're seeing Peggy at Neiman's, right?"

"Yes, why do you ask?"

"Well, I was hoping I could ask you a few questions about Billy Matlin while you're here. Peggy told us you were seeing her and I wondered if you'd had any run-ins with Billy of late."

His face darkened. "Oh, him? What makes you think I had anything to do with his disappearance?"

He rubbed a large palm over his bear-like face. "Sure, we had words the other day, but I never laid a hand on that crazy man."

"Crazy?"

"Yeah, what kind of man goes around telling everyone that they're seeing Bigfoot in the woods? Much better to keep that sort of thing quiet."

That got my attention. "Oh, and does that mean you've seen Bigfoot firsthand?"

"Not exactly, but I've sure seen something big crossing US 23 before. I wasn't close enough to say what it was for sure, but it wasn't a deer or bear. I can well imagine how stories get out, and many of us here in East Tawas have been on the lookout for the infamous beast. The stories in the newspaper didn't help either, but when Billy approached me in the Walmart parking lot, he went on about how he was trying to prove that Bigfoot was real, and how he hoped that when he found him, he'd be rich. He would have more than enough money to pay up his child support and then some."

"Why was he telling you that and not his ex, Peggy?"

"She refused to talk to him or let him see the kids until he came up with the money to pay his support."

"That's not good. He still deserves to see his children, regardless."

He nodded. "I told Peggy that once, but she said Billy had his kids out in the wood helping him look for Bigfoot. She felt that he was placing them in danger and was more determined than ever to keep the kids away from him until he came to his senses."

"So the support money wasn't the only reason she kept her children away?"

"Nope."

"If she doesn't believe Bigfoot is real, what danger would the kids be in out in the woods with Billy?"

"There still might be bears and cougars out there."

"Cougars? You know, the DNR says there aren't any in Michigan."

"That's what they keep on saying, but that's not the truth. I found a deer carcass in a tree not long ago. What kind of animal puts a carcass in a tree besides a big cat like a cougar?"

"Beats me," Eleanor said. "I suppose I can't blame Peggy if she thought the kids might be in danger, but I can't help but think there's more to it."

"Like what?" I asked.

"Like that Peggy knows Billy isn't as nuts as she says. What if she actually saw Bigfoot herself, and that's the real reason she picked up and left?"

We both looked at Bubba until he said, "If she did, she certainly didn't tell me. I never put a hand on Billy, but I did tell him that if he ever wanted to see the kids again, he needed to put an end to this Bigfoot thing."

"What did he say to that?"

"Nothing. He just left and I haven't seen him since. I was surprised when Peggy told me the sheriff had stopped by asking questions about Billy."

"So, what do you think really happened to Billy?"

"I'm not sure, but I can't imagine the man just dropped off the face of the planet. He might still be in the woods searching for Bigfoot, unless the hairy beast got him."

"I see. Well, I'm just not buying that. If Billy ran into Bigfoot in the woods, I'm sure both beast and man would put distance between themselves. I don't think Bigfoot wants to be found."

"So you think a man hell bent on finding Bigfoot would run away if he actually found him?"

"I can't say. I was just running a scenario by you." He eyed my car, looking under the hood. "It seems like your battery cables have fallen off. How on earth did that happen?"

"I wanted to have a legitimate reason for talking to you. Peggy said we shouldn't go to Randy's Towing since you just started working there."

He pulled a wrench out of his pocket and refastened the cables to the battery posts. "Next time, just call me." He rattled off his cell number, which I added to my contact list in my cell phone. I then thanked the man, climbing back into the car and we followed the wrecker to US 23, parting ways. When the light changed, I parked in the state dock's parking lot.

An Animal Channel van was parked there and El and I exited the car and sauntered over to them. Two men were downing sandwiches when we rounded the van. They stood next to the van, chatting with a blonde with wild hair. My eyes widened when it was Rosa Lee Hill.

"Hey, Agnes and Eleanor. Did you know that Mike and Chad are here to interview Billy Matlin?"

Before I had a chance to answer, one of the men informed us; "We were. Until Sheriff Peterson stopped by and questioned us about the missing Billy Matlin."

"Chad, the sheriff told us not to tell anyone he questioned us, remember?"

"Sure, Mike, but since when have you known me to let the cops tell me what to do?"

"Exactly. What did the sheriff want to know?"

"Not much, just wondered when the last time we might have seen Billy Matlin," Chad said.

"Oh, have you interviewed Billy already?"

"We had planned to yesterday, but Brent from the Animal Network told us Billy had disappeared."

That got my attention. "Really! And he told you this yesterday, not today?"

"Yes," Chad said. "I was surprised because I had spoken with Billy on the phone yesterday in the morning."

"Thanks for that bit of information. Did you get the impression that the Animal Network was trying to get the exclusive?"

Mike laughed. "Like their network will ever make it off the ground."

"So why did you listen to them and not find out firsthand where Billy was?" I asked.

"I did call, but he never returned my call. I had planned to run out to his house today to see if we could touch base with him."

"But the sheriff stopped us before we had the chance and told us he was investigating Billy's disappearance now," Mike added.

"I'm Private Eye, Agnes Barton, and this is my partner Eleanor Mason. Billy hired us to find Bigfoot, and ever since things have gotten hairy."

"Pun intended," Eleanor added. "The Department of Natural Resources and the United States Fish and Wildlife Service have taken DNA samples of hair that might belong to Bigfoot."

Mike's eyes widened. "And what were their findings?"

I shrugged. "Beats me. They're still fighting amongst themselves, but now they're trying to deal with all the big game hunters who have rolled into East Tawas this morning. It seems that everyone wants a piece of Bigfoot, and some who want him in pieces."

"Then there's the prize money that has been put up by an investor," El said.

"Hopefully, that bit of news isn't coming from the Animal

Network people. I wouldn't believe anything they say," Chad said.

"So, you don't believe it? Isn't that what your show, *Finding Bigfoot*, is all about?"

"That's different. We're legitimate."

"We shouldn't be jumping to conclusions just yet. Who knows, the Animal Network might be the next big thing," I said. *Yeah, I* thought, *perhaps if they lost Brent, that is.*

"I guess that might just be a job for our legal department."

"Legal department?" a loud voice asked behind me.

I whirled in time to see my intended, Andrew Hart, looking fetching in white pants and a crew T-shirt that billowed in the wind. His gray hair was slicked back and my heart skipped a beat.

I did a quick introduction and Chad went on to say, "For one thing, the name Animal Network is too similar to Animal Channel, and we have *Finding Bigfoot* with prize money being offered and they have *Hunting Bigfoot*. So, I guess you can see the problem."

"Yes, you're jelly," Eleanor said. "Younger folks' word for jealous."

"What do we have to be jealous about? Everyone knows the Animal Channel has the best shows around."

"Huh!" Eleanor spat. "They did when most of the shows were about animals, but these days reality shows have overtaken the channel."

"Not true. We still have lion week."

I waved my arms to halt this barrage of insults. "That's about enough. You both have solid points, but the only thing important to me is to find Billy Matlin right now."

"And Bigfoot," Eleanor added. "We have a way better chance at it than either of you. We'll be on that reality show and will be able to see first-hand what the Animal Network is all about when we hunt for Bigfoot."

Andrew's brow shot up. "Is that right, Agnes? Are you really planning to tromp around in the woods with your bad hip?"

"It's been doing much better these days."

He swiped a hand through his hair. "We'll talk about this later."

"Sure, after I ask Brent a few questions first."

Eleanor stared at the sky that was becoming darker now. "We might need to do that back at my place. It's almost dark and I missed dinner."

I thanked Chad and Mike, and then Eleanor and I went back to the car. Andrew pulled me close, I thought for a quick kiss, but he said in my ear, "I'll meet you back at Eleanor's, and if truth be known, I'm dead set against you and Eleanor going near that reality show. You're—"

"I'm perfectly aware that I'm seventy-two, Andrew. All I know is that I need to get to the bottom of this before someone else mysteriously disappears."

"I insist on tagging along, then."

"I'm not sure the host, Brent, will allow it, but Rosa Lee Hill's boys Curt and Curtis will be there, and they're more than enough protection if you ask me."

"That doesn't mean I won't be there, even if they don't allow me on set. I'll be there in spirit."

I shrugged. "Knock yourself out." I quickly changed the subject. "So what brings you back to East Tawas so soon? I thought you had a big case back in Detroit."

"I did, but I was able to resolve it pretty quickly."

"Why is it you know more about what's going on with me than I do you?"

He rubbed his chin. "Probably because I don't talk about my cases like you do. I take client attorney privilege seriously. I assure you, it's nothing nearly as exciting as what you and Eleanor are doing."

I smiled a bit, but I just wished I knew more about his cases. I mean, for all I knew he might be representing serial killers. Then I remembered, this is Michigan and I can't recall the last time a real serial killer roamed the state. But then again, you just never know.

"Perhaps it might be better if you settled in at the Days Inn since Eleanor and I need to discuss our case."

"Are you trying to get rid of me?"

"Not at all. I just don't want to bore you with the details."

"You mean you don't want me to know what's really going on."

I fanned my face as I reached the car. Eleanor was already in the car and I was so trying to get rid of Andrew for the time being. "There's nothing more to say. We're looking for Bigfoot is all. Billy Matlin hired us and now he's gone missing. I'm more determined than ever to find out the truth."

"Let me get this straight. You're actually looking for Bigfoot?"

"Yes, but more importantly, this show will give us the chance to look for Billy since he's disappeared without a trace."

"I see. So … are you buying into this Bigfoot thing is the question?"

I took in a breath. "Actually, yes. It seems just about everyone in town claimed to have seen something suspicious in the woods or crossing US 23. There's too many to say that they are all nuts."

"Okay, fine. I'll go book a room at Days Inn, but you need to tell me where this show is being taped so I can be there tomorrow."

I nodded and told him what he wanted to know, secretly wishing he'd change his mind and not show up in the morning. Once Andrew and I had parted, I slid behind wheel and all but ignored Eleanor who merely exchanged a glance with me. I started the car and headed back to Eleanor's house, not allowing Andrew to cloud my judgment. That's the last thing I needed right now.

I whipped into Eleanor's drive fast enough to scatter stones. We went inside and Eleanor rummaged in her refrigerator, coming back with leftover roasted chicken. I just shook my head since the last thing on my mind was food.

I accepted a soda from Eleanor, not wanting to voice my concerns about tomorrow, until she said, "So, what do you make of Brent telling those Animal Channel guys that Billy Matlin was missing a day before he actually was?"

I popped the lid of the cold can, taking a sip. "Well, there might be a few reasons for that. He might have wanted to stall them from interviewing Billy."

"Just like we were."

"That was for a much different reason. I wanted to buy us some time while the wildlife people tested the samples they found. Brent wanted to most likely keep it quiet so that his show got all the attention."

"I guess neither of those things happened and that interview with Animal Channel never happened."

I sauntered to the patio door and opened the sliding glass door, making my way to a patio chair. As I sat, Eleanor joined me and we gazed at the orange and pink sky as the sun had nearly set.

"Billy had been doing interviews for the local newspapers, though, and the Bigfoot story seemed to spread like wildfire. It's too late to wait for testing results now. It's apparent that big game hunters are here to stay, which makes me very nervous."

"Yeah," Eleanor said. "I sure hope we don't get shot in the woods while we do that reality show, but I'm sure Sheriff Peterson will get a handle on the situation. He won't allow East Tawas to be turned upside down."

"Right. Plus, with the DNR and U.S. Fish and Game Service also involved, they'll take care of it. Bigfoot isn't a known Michigan game animal."

"It probably wouldn't hurt for us to talk to those guys again. We don't even know if they finally decided to get off their laurels and test that brown hair."

I yawned. "We'll do that, but remember, tomorrow we have to be on the set of the reality show, and I would love to speak to the wildlife people for sure." I took another swig of my soda and stretched. "I'm heading home now. I need to hit the hay early tonight so I can be ready for the show tomorrow."

With a wave, I wandered back inside and out the door. As I drove home, it occurred to me that I never received a phone call from Martha or Sophia. I'd just give them a call when I got home. I slowed the car down as it was quite dark now. I used the high beams when I could, which was when a car wasn't coming from the opposite direction. Besides, you just never knew when a white-tailed deer might just dart in front of the car. At my age, my reaction times are much slower and the last thing I needed was to have a deer crashing through my windshield. I'm pretty sure that would give me a heart attack for sure.

I rounded the last bend before my place, and when I was finally in the driveway, I rolled to a stop as close to my door as possible. I cut off the engine, got out, and my heart went to pounding. I breathed deeply of the marigolds I had planted in my flowerbeds, but I had the strange feeling something just wasn't right. It was also too silent for my liking. I had no idea if it was all the hoopla about Bigfoot that I was feeling, but I can't remember a night that was so silent. Even though my sensor lights flashed on, I still didn't feel at ease. I craned an ear, but not even a cricket chirped.

I rustled my keys, cramming my door key in the lock and turned it quickly, shouldering open the door. Once I was inside, I slammed the door closed and locked it. Within the glow of the light over my sink that I always kept on, two glowing eyes made their way toward me from the hallway. I dropped my purse with a clunk, gripping my heart with one hand until I heard, "Meow."

Oh, thank the Lord. It was my cat, Duchess. I swooped her up and gave her a good scratching under her chin. She nuzzled my chin with her nose and I made my way into the kitchen, flipping on the lights. I set Duchess down and filled her bowls with food and fresh water. It was then that I saw the flashing red light on my answering machine.

I walked over and pressed the message button. "Mother. I've been trying, like, *forever* to get a hold of you. Call me when you get this message." Click.

I called Martha back right away and she berated me for not answering my cell phone. "Sorry," I said. "It hasn't been ringing and I can't figure out how to fix it."

Martha gave me instructions on how to turn the ringer on. "I really should buy you that *iPhone For Seniors* book. You know, it's one of those 'For Dummies' books."

"Right after I get you the 'how to call your mother for dummies' book."

"Look, that's not why I called. I just wanted you to know that your great-granddaughter is in the hospital with flu-like symptoms. Poor Andrea was quite dehydrated and is still running a fever. Sophia is at the hospital with Bill at her side, but he's leaving for home soon. They'll be taking turns sitting with her. I don't think I've ever seen Bill so rattled before."

"Oh? Are they allowing him the time off from work?"

"Yes, a few days anyway. Sophia sure could use some help, so I'm not going to the reality show shoot tomorrow. Peyton can find himself another assistant for all I care. Family comes first."

I couldn't believe she was saying that, but I was sure happy to see her stand up for Sophia like that.

"I'll drop by the hospital before we go to the shoot. If I had known she was admitted to the hospital I would have been there, too."

"Don't worry about it, Mother. The nursing staff is limiting who is allowed to see her right now. It seems there have been some outbreaks of the flu of late, and they're asking that children and the elderly not visit patients at this time."

"Elderly?" I spat. "I can't believe that. If anyone tries to stop me from visiting, I'll sick Eleanor on them."

"Seriously, Mother. I'll look after her. If Andrea's condition changes, I'll call you."

Martha hung up and I had a sick feeling in the pit of my stomach. I just can't believe that I can't visit my own grandbaby, but I suppose the hospital is only trying to protect the patients, and probably us. I was always quite diligent about getting my flu shot every year, though. I made a quick call and told Eleanor the news and she spouted off about as much as I had, but I assured her we'd sneak in if Andrea didn't get better in a few days. Before I hung up with Eleanor, I reminded her to lock all of her doors.

"Come on, Duchess," I said. "Let's head to bed. I'm bushed."

Duchess bounded up the hallway with me following. I changed

and slipped between the cool sheets, with Duchess snuggling next to me. It didn't take me long to nod off.

Chapter Fourteen

I woke up to the sound of my front door being pounded on. Somehow, the vibration made its way up the hallway and into my rattled brain. I begrudgingly swung my legs out from beneath my warm covers and slid my feet into my slippers, padding my way up the hallway and peeked through the curtains.

I opened the door and Andrew walked in, carrying a Tim Horton's box—filled with yummy donuts, I hoped.

"What brings you by so early?"

"Because I know you so well. If I don't come with you to that reality show that's starting today, you'll duck me for sure."

"Since when do you want to be involved in my investigations?"

He busied himself in the kitchen making coffee. "I don't exactly, but I'm curious. It can't hurt to have an attorney on site to look over any documents they want you to sign."

"We already signed something, but it had to do with liability."

"So basically, if you or Eleanor drop dead while filming, it releases them from liability?"

"Something like that, but I'm sure it's a standard form."

"Perhaps not. I can't imagine they usually have participants your ages."

"Is that a crack about my age, mister?"

"Of course not. I'm your age, or have you forgotten?"

"Yes, but men are allowed to be older. People don't treat women the same way as we age."

"Aww, they're just jealous because women live longer, is all. Men die much quicker when they run around with younger women," he winked.

I gave him a sock in his shoulder. "Not funny, mister."

"I was just kidding, anyway. You should know I'm not like that. I would much rather spend my time with a confident older woman any day of the week."

"Just as long as they aren't investigators, isn't that right?"

He bit into a chocolate donut. "Sorry, guilty as charged, but it's not like you listen to me. I'm not so much against it as worried about you and Eleanor. Neither of you are spring chickens."

"I know, but I'm just at the point in my life where I want to be a doer, not a sit-on-the-rocking-chair-all-day rocker."

"Go ahead and get dressed while I fetch Eleanor. It might be quicker that way."

I padded up the hallway and into the bathroom.

An hour later, Eleanor was sitting at the table munching on donuts. She was dressed in the camouflage clothing we bought the other day. I was similarly dressed and reached for the donut box, but my face fell when there weren't any donuts left that I liked. "Didn't you get peanut crunch donuts?" I asked Andrew.

His eyes widened for a moment, and then he said, "They didn't have any."

My eyes darted to Eleanor who was promptly brushing nut crumbs off the table. "Thanks, Eleanor."

"I can't help it if I like them, too."

"But you also know that they're my favorite."

"Are you two going to fight about donuts all day, or should we leave for the show now?" Andrew asked with a guilty look on his face, no doubt because he was caught in a lie.

I glared at the nearly empty coffee pot. I poured the remainder in a cup, topping it off with vanilla creamer. I quickly stirred it in and Andrew came over and planted a kiss on my neck. "Sorry, Aggie. I should have saved a peanut crunch for you."

I took a sip with a shaking hand. "It's not the donut, or barely getting a cup of coffee. I'm just worried about Sophia's baby. She was admitted to the hospital and Martha told me that I wouldn't be allowed to visit, something to do with a flu outbreak."

"Not to worry. Why not call Martha this morning before we leave? That way you won't be worrying all day. Perhaps the baby is doing better this morning."

I called Martha and she told me the fever broke, but Andrea was still quite sick. Bill took Sophia home and Martha was staying at the hospital until he returned. It had taken him over two hours to convince Sophia that he was quite capable of looking after Andrea, and that she needed rest or she'd be the next one hospitalized.

"Oh, my," I said. "Thanks, Martha, for giving me an update. I sure hope the baby makes a full recovery, and soon."

When I hung up, I cut off the power to the coffee pot, and gave Duchess a quick pat before heading out the door. We settled ourselves in the car, and I was more than a little surprised that not only did Andrew not insist on driving, but he sat in the back seat.

I drove to the Cat Lady's house, and there were few cars in the driveway, which made me wonder what was going on? We got out of the car, and made our way to the door. Brent opened the door and he looked a fright. His dark hair stuck up and there were dark circles beneath his eyes.

He opened the door enough for us to come inside and I had to ask, "What's going on here?"

"Those damn Animal Channel people are what! They filed an injunction to halt the show. They're claiming they own the copyright to Bigfoot shows. What a joke. They're trying to say there are trademark issues, and that even the Animal Network name is under dispute."

"I'd love to see the paperwork on that one," Andrew said. "I'm an attorney and Agnes's fiancé."

"Sounds good to me. We haven't had the funds to retain an attorney."

He handed Andrew the documents, and Andrew pulled out a pair of reading glasses, going over the paperwork at the table.

"Have you spoken to the Animal Channel people recently?" I asked.

"No."

"Really? That's strange, since they told us just yesterday that you had."

"Yeah," Eleanor said. "Did you really tell them that Billy Matlin went missing a whole day before he actually did?"

Brent's face hardened. "Fine, so I did; but I was just trying to prevent Billy from doing that interview. We're having a hard enough time giving our show the push it needs. That interview would have further complicated matters."

"What do you know about Billy Matlin's disappearance?" I asked.

"Nothing except for what I'd been told—that his place was in shambles, and no Billy to be found."

"Did you have anything to do with Billy disappearing?" I pressed.

"Of course not! I just made up the story about Billy being missing."

Eleanor huffed. "Oh, so it was just a strange coincidence, is that it?"

"I suppose. I was just as surprised as anyone else in town."

"What makes you think anyone was surprised by his disappearance?"

"I'm not sure. Why wouldn't it be a surprise? I can't image anyone in town would expect for him to go missing."

"Except that he's kind of a nut case in town. I don't think anyone really believed his stories. I bet most folks in town might think that he's just wandering in the woods."

"True, Aggie," Eleanor said. "But that wouldn't explain the broken patio window."

"If only we could find out if the blood found was Billy's, or even human."

"We could ask Sheriff Peterson, but I doubt he's going to tell us."

"Right. Where did you say you were from, Brent?"

"I didn't, but I'm originally from Ashton, North Carolina. I grew up around the mountains most of my life."

"And when did you become so interested in Bigfoot?"

He rubbed his arm and said, "Most of my life. I love animals and I couldn't help but notice the signs that were out in the wilderness areas where folks claimed to have seen Bigfoot."

"Signs?" Eleanor asked. "What kind of signs?"

"Broken tree branches where there shouldn't be any … scat."

"Oh," I said. "I never thought about that. Have you ever seen an actual Bigfoot before?"

"I've smelled it and seen signs on the trail, but I never faced one down if that's what you're asking."

Andrew handed back the paperwork. "This is just a process. There's a hearing in a few days. They certainly can't establish that no other show can be called Animal anything. You're the Animal Network, not close enough for them to claim violations of a trademark. The *Hunting Bigfoot* is similar to *Finding Bigfoot*, but that would depend on how similar your show is to theirs."

"We're taking in a team of newbies, not professionals like they have. We're trying to gauge how participants react on a real Bigfoot hunt. This area has already been proven to be active in that regard."

"I see. Well, that certainly sounds much different from their show. I'd be happy to handle the court proceedings, but I recommend that you try to reason with them before that hearing. I'm sure they don't want a lengthy legal battle. They might also look like a bunch of bullies. I'd be happy to mediate on your behalf."

"That sounds great. If you could hang out for a while, we could work on a plan together."

Andrew gave me a hug. "I hope you don't mind, Agnes. I'd really like to help these guys out. I haven't done a pro-bono in quite a while."

"You're not charging us?" Brent asked. "Is this for real?"

"Sure it is. I like to help out fledglings like yourselves."

"Do you have any more questions, Agnes?" Brent asked.

"Not at all. We'll be in touch. We'd like to question the wildlife guys, though, to see if they tested that animal hair yet."

Andrew stayed behind to help out Brent, but Eleanor and I left, and once we were back in the car, Eleanor said, "Do you believe that Brent made up the whole disappearance of Billy thing?"

"I'm not really sure, but we can come back to it if we receive any information that might link him to Billy Matlin."

"Besides, it wasn't in anyone's best interest for Billy to talk to the Animal Channel."

"Doesn't matter, I suppose. Billy got his word out, regardless of if it was the Animal Channel or the local press. There's no turning back now. I just wish I could figure out what really happened to Billy. His ex-wife certainly didn't shed any light on the situation, and neither did her boyfriend, Bubba. It makes no sense to me that either of them would wish Billy harm since they were counting on that child support money to start rolling in soon."

"Look; Billy didn't have a job to pay child support, and I can't imagine either of them expecting that Billy would just somehow fall into a pile of money to make things right. For Billy, things ran much deeper than that," Eleanor pointed out.

"Okay, so either someone is lying, or someone else meant harm to Billy."

"Someone who went to quite a bit of trouble covering it up," Eleanor added. "What's our next plan of action?"

"Interview the DNR and U.S. Fish and Wildlife Service like I mentioned earlier."

Chapter Fifteen

I drove thru town, which was in full swing of summer, but all the guys and gals dressed in camouflage sure stuck out. At least they weren't armed to the gills now. "It seems like Sheriff Peterson was handling the gun-toting hunters for the time being."

"Why do you say that, Agnes?"

"Well, I don't see any rifles and shotguns."

"True, but they most likely have them packed away and out of sight. My bet is they'd be back out in a millisecond if someone spotted anything that looks like Bigfoot."

"Luckily, the only sightings have been outside of town."

We strode on the state dock when a sail caught my attention. It had a picture of Bigfoot with the wordage, "Hunting Bigfoot."

I couldn't help but stare widely at the huge yacht. We were used to seeing some huge boats and yachts moored at the dock, but we were led to believe that this small Animal Network didn't even have funds enough to retain an attorney.

"Maybe the Animal Network is doing much better than they let on," Eleanor observed.

"I'd sure like to ask Brent the next time we see him, though."

Just then, two men surfaced from below deck. One of them was Peyton Daniels, the director of *Hunting Bigfoot*. He waved and approached the dock while the other man hung back.

"Hello there, Agnes. Sorry about the show, but we'll be back on track shortly."

I gazed up at the sails. "That's some yacht. I had no idea that the Animal Network was this big an operation."

"Yeah," Eleanor butted in. "Brent told us—"

"Nothing. He told us nothing," I interjected. "We just thought the Animal Network was a smaller operation, is all."

"Not really. I mean we have some worthwhile investors. *Hunting Bigfoot* will be the first show in a series of animal based shows."

"Oh?" I said. "Is your network going to consist of all reality shows?"

"Not at all. We have an oceanographer that will be doing underwater exploration similar to Jacques Cousteau. He's not only a conservationist, but a filmmaker."

"I see. Well, I'd love to meet him sometime," I said, eyeing the man on the yacht. "Is that him?"

The short man came forward and invited us onboard. "How delightful to meet more locals. I'm Pierre DePaul."

Eleanor and I boarded the yacht with the help of Peyton. "Please, follow me below deck. There're a few other ladies on board that are also going to be on the *Hunting Bigfoot* show."

We descended the steps that led into a large room with white leather couches that came in three sections, each positioned around a small table in the center. Three women glanced up when we walked toward them. Eleanor's sister, Margarita, waved shyly. "Hello, girls. Fancy meeting you here."

Eleanor's eyes swept from Margarita, to Tammy Rodrigue and her friend, Dixie. At least Tammy didn't have her bow with her.

"What are you doing here, Margarita?" Eleanor asked.

Tammy's eyes narrowed. "The same reason as you, I suspect, but we got here first so you two can shoo. We're handling this end of the investigation."

Of all the nerve! Who did this young lady think she was, anyway? "Oh, and what qualifies you as an investigator?"

Tammy leaned forward. "For one, we solved a case back in Bear Paw."

"Did you now? Well, let me just tell you that this isn't Bear Paw and Eleanor and I don't need any help with the investigation. We were hired by Billy Matlin, and all you're doing here is competing in a reality show."

"Well, since Billy has gone missing, I guess that means you're out of a job."

I had half a mind to turn this young lady over my knee because I didn't care for her mouth a bit. "Hardly! We're investigating his disappearance, which will be way harder since the reality show has been temporarily halted."

"That will be cleared up soon enough," Pierre said, "just as soon as my team of attorneys arrives from England. I'm well connected."

"That's nice, but my fiancé is an attorney and is working with Brent on the matter. He's suggested that the Animal Network should meet with the Animal Channel people to resolve the matter. I'm sure together they can come up with a resolution without a huge court case."

"I see. Well, I'm all for resolving this sooner rather than later." Pierre turned to Peyton. "Give Brent a call and see what gives."

Peyton moved to a gold telephone and made his call while Pierre offered us beverages. A uniformed young man came forward dressed in all white and nodded when Pierre asked him to fetch a bottle of wine.

I shook my head. "Wine? Isn't it awfully early for that?"

"In France, it matters not what time of the day it is. Peter will bring us some nice brie and crackers. It's never a good thing to drink on an empty stomach, if that's what you're worried about, Agnes."

"I didn't tell you my name."

"I've invested a good sum of money to know who I'm dealing with. Peyton told me all about you and your friend, Eleanor. I'm confident that you'll make a great addition to our little reality show."

The wine was brought and the cork popped and passed around so that everyone could take a whiff, which brought a smile to Eleanor's face. "We're not used to this sort of thing. We're simple folks here in Michigan."

"Simple?"

"Yes, not used to wine this early, or the charming company of a foreigner."

I nudged Eleanor. "Perhaps we should skip the wine, Eleanor. You know wine goes straight to your head."

"Speak for yourself. I'll be just fine." She stared at the brie that had been set down. "I'm not so sure about this, though. I'm more used to Cheese Whiz."

"She's joking," I said.

Margarita took the wine glass that was handed to her. "Oh, my. I can't even remember the last time I've had wine this fancy." She took a sip and giggled.

Tammy looked down at her wine glass. "Is this all I get? This is only a shot," she said as she tipped it back, causing Dixie to giggle.

"You just kill me, Tammy."

Eleanor's eyes widened. "Never good to say that word in this town. Every time someone does, someone dies. The thing is, we just never expected Billy to just disappear like that. We can't figure out what might have happened. It was really so unexpected."

"I haven't dealt with any missing persons cases yet," Tammy admitted. "But we'd be more than happy to help out if you'd like."

I smiled. "Thanks, but Eleanor and I work solo."

Eleanor nodded. "We'd sure like to know more about Brent though, Pierre. What can you tell us about him?"

Pierre paused in thought. "Peyton could answer that question better than I could."

Peyton cradled his wine glass in his hand. "Well, I met Brent in Ashton, North Carolina. He was quite the loudmouth and was telling the locals how he was investigating Bigfoot in the mountains. Well, to be honest, I thought the man was crazy as Cracker Jacks, but after I bought him a pitcher of beer we began talking, and I went out on a limb and went back to his house where he claimed he had proof that what he was saying wasn't just a story."

"So, he was trying to pick you up?" Eleanor asked with a smile.

"That's what I thought at first, but once we got to his place, he had maps, pictures, and vocal recordings. To be honest, I was quite impressed with his attention to detail."

"Did you ever go out and look for Bigfoot together?"

"We sure did, but we never found any signs. I spent the whole week in the mountains, but it was clear that whatever had been out there had moved on."

"Is that what you think Bigfoot does—changes location so as not to be detected?"

"With everything I've seen thus far, I'd have to say yes. We've been following Bigfoot's trails ever since, but after a particularly grueling night of chasing noises out in the mountains, we ran across Pierre. He had gotten himself lost in the North Carolina mountains."

"True story," Pierre said. "If it hadn't been for Brent and Peyton, I'd probably have succumbed to the elements. Later, when Peyton told me about what they were doing out in the mountains, I just thought it might be a great show. I've been exploring the oceans for quite some time, but there's just something about Bigfoot that has always interested me."

"I suppose you were one of those men who searched for mermaids, too," Eleanor said.

"I won't lie. I sure have, and that research has led me to rally against your government which continues to test sonar, endangering the marine life."

"I've read about that," I said. "We're you ever able to do anything about that?"

"I'm still involved, but my group had to disband when the government took all of the data we'd collected, including our underwater recordings. I felt like I had been singled out, so I decided to invest my funds in a channel that would be able to show the public more than just a conservation group."

"Wouldn't hunting Bigfoot hurt your credibility?"

"At this point, I don't care. I'm more of a silent partner for the time being, until I can really get the channel off the ground. I just hadn't planned for the Animal Channel to try to stop us on every turn. I really can't see why they have worried so much since we're so small, but I suppose they don't want to risk any real competition."

"Hogwash," Eleanor said. "They're just trying to bully you, is all. If the public knew what was happening, you might be able to resolve this situation quicker than you hoped. I just hate how a big channel like the Animal Channel would try to hurt a fledging, but I'm sure if it were public knowledge, they'd back down in a heartbeat."

"Eleanor's right, but this matter needs to be handled right."

"Which is what I plan to do. Peyton, what did Brent say?"

"That the Animal Channel would meet us tomorrow to discuss the matter."

"Great. If you ladies would excuse us, we really need to take care of this. Perhaps you could stop by another time."

Eleanor and I followed Margarita, Tammy, and Dixie off the yacht and back onto the dock. "Well," Margarita said. "I can't imagine you learned anything to help with your case, have you, Eleanor?"

"Nope, but at least we know the whole story about how and where the Animal Network came from."

"True, Eleanor, but now we don't have any leads to follow." Eleanor opened her mouth, but snapped it closed when I gave her one of my famous looks. "We'll be in touch," I told Margarita as Eleanor and I whirled away.

When we were out of hearing distance of the Margarita and her friends, Eleanor said, "I sure hope my sister and her friends don't interfere in our investigation."

"I'm not worried, but it's better to not divulge too many details. We still have the wildlife people to question, if only we can figure out where they'd be. I had hoped they'd be at the state dock for some reason. Where else could they be?"

"Sheriff's department? Whitetail Cafe?"

"So you actually think they'd be at the Whitetail Cafe?"

"It's almost noon now. I'm hungry. That brie stuff was tasteless."

I smiled. "Well, you certainly learned to mask your reactions, Eleanor. I guess by now, we've both learned a thing or two about investigating crimes."

Chapter Sixteen

Eleanor and I strolled back to the parking lot, but we froze when we saw a sign that read 'Bigfoot Xing' on the wall of the bait shop near the dock. I made tracks over there.

Eleanor tried to catch up. "What on earth, Aggie?"

I pointed out the sign and she said, "Oh."

We entered the small bait shop that had tanks of minnows alongside one wall that snapped and popped as bubbles burst to the surface of the tank. The weathered walls were covered with nostalgic metal signs, advertising all sorts of old fashioned products, from gasoline stations to Ivory soap.

I made my way to the cash register where a rope hung from the ceiling with yellow caps with the words, *Hunting Bigfoot* in black lettering. There were also diamond-shaped signs affixed to the walls behind the register with 'Bigfoot Xing' like I'd seen outside— presumably for sale.

A young man was working behind the counter, totally ignoring us as he was currently texting on his iPhone.

"Ahem," I said to get his attention.

When he looked up, I smiled. "How's the fishing today?"

"Not much off the dock today. There's a pocket near Big Charity Island, but you have to have a boat to get there, unless you get a spot on a charter boat. They find even better spots to fish."

"I sure miss the old days," I said. "You could get plenty of perch right off the dock. Back in those days, the dock was packed with fishermen."

The young man ran a hand through his closely-shorn blond hair.

"That's what my grandpa said, but there are still times when you can catch fish off the dock. You just have to figure out when they're really biting, is all."

Enough small talk, so I asked, "What's up with all the Bigfoot signs?"

"It's the big news lately. Folks claim to have seen something that most of them think is Bigfoot. Two channels in town are working on the story, too. One of them is shooting a reality show from what I hear."

"Oh, I might have heard something about that. How about you? What do you make of the stories?"

He shrugged. "Anything is possible, I suppose. There are plenty of spots around here where Bigfoot or other large animals might be lurking."

"Have you ever seen Bigfoot first-hand?"

"I'm not that crazy, and if I did see something I'd keep it to myself. I'm about ready to join the Marines and I don't need them thinking I'm psychologically off."

"Thanks for your dedication to our country in advance. We're trying to investigate the incidences and I just wonder if it's all just a tall tale."

"Might be, but I heard that Billy Matlin went missing. Most folks think Bigfoot got him."

"Really? But there isn't any solid evidence that Bigfoot even exists from my recollection."

"Nope, but something mighty strange has been seen crossing US 23. Also there are some houses secluded in the woods near the Matlin place where home owners have reported some strange incidences."

"Like what?" Eleanor asked with widened eyes.

"Scratching on their doors and windows at night. One lady told me when she looked out her window she saw a hairy beast looking in at her!"

Eleanor pressed a fist to her breast. "How scary. Did she call the cops at least?"

"She called her husband, and he came right home. From what I heard, Sheriff Peterson went out there to check things out."

I pulled out a notebook from my purse. "Can you give me the name of the lady who told you the story?"

He sighed. "I'm not sure if I should. I mean she was pretty shaken up about the incident. She might not like it if I mention her name."

"I understand, but we're investigators Agnes Barton and Eleanor Mason, and we've had a devil of a time trying to investigate this case. You see, Billy Matlin hired us to find Bigfoot, and when he went missing, we became even more driven to find out the truth."

"Aren't you two awfully up there in years to be tromping out in the woods?"

I smiled. "We're paid up on our health insurance, and we're extra careful. Besides, right now we've been just questioning people who claimed to have seen Bigfoot. Our hope is that somehow we'll run across someone that might know what happened to Billy, or even find him."

"Billy might have just gone deeper into the woods and got himself lost," Eleanor added.

"I doubt that. He used to be special ops and has real survival skills," the young man said.

I shook my head to clear my reeling mind. "I sure don't see him like that. He sure has let himself go."

"Some claim he was exposed to chemical weapons during the Gulf war. He hasn't been right ever since. Even before he was hunting Bigfoot he was on the odd side. Some thought that's why he was discharged from the Marines."

"I see. Well, did you know him personally?"

"Nope. My mom told me to stay away from him. My family is very pro-military and I suspect they were worried that Billy might scare me away from joining up when I came of age."

"So enlisting is always something you have wanted to do?"

"Yes, since I was about twelve. My dad and granddad were also Marines. It's fitting that I join up, too."

"If that's what you want out of life. You can't beat earning money for college and medical insurance. I hope you stay safe."

I turned to leave and we almost made it to the door when the young man said, "Shelly Niles. That's the woman who told me Bigfoot was looking in her window. She lives out on Lincoln Street."

We thanked the young man for the information and ran straight into Tammy Rodrigue outside. I locked eyes with her and she asked, "Did you find out any information in there?"

"Nope, another dead end."

"Why not join forces? We can cover more ground that way."

"Sounds good. Why don't you check out Billy Matlin's place again and see if Billy showed back up at home?" I rattled off the address and she grinned as she jotted it down.

We waved at Margarita and Dixie who were also waiting outside. Eleanor and I drove off five minutes later, and as I made the turn onto US 23, Eleanor asked, "Why did you send them over to Billy's place? I thought you didn't want them on our investigation."

"I don't, but I know if I didn't give them something to do that they'd just go in the bait shop and ask that young man about what he just told us."

"Well, they don't know the area as well, so it's doubtful they'd be able to find the place."

"True, but you can find out just about anything online these days, like where someone lives with just a name. Scary, actually."

Within ten minutes, we were on Lincoln Street near the airport. I drove past white pines that bordered the street on either side. This was a rural residential area where houses were few and far between.

"Stop, Aggie," Eleanor said, pointing out a large mailbox with the name Niles in bold letters.

I made the turn, making my way up the long, narrow drive that widened a half mile up. There was a barnwood-sided two-story house with a covered, homemade carport of sorts to the left. Large tree trunks held up the makeshift roof with shingles thrown on the top. I highly doubted it would keep moisture off any vehicle parked there, or be able to hold much snow without the possibility of collapsing.

El and I clamored out and walked cautiously to the door, rapping gently on it. It made me more than a little nervous. You just never know if your sudden appearance at a stranger's door might have them pulling out the shotgun. I didn't believe this was normal for most folks around here, but I, for one, would be too nervous to live this far out in the sticks.

The sound of barking dogs and excitement of children could be heard when the door was opened a crack. One brown eye locked with mine, and as it softened, the door was opened to reveal a mousy woman of about thirty, dressed in a floral dress in subdued colors of cream and light pink.

"Can I help you?" she asked in a soft-spoken voice.

A dark-haired child poked his head out the door. "Who is it, Mama?"

She pushed him back inside and the barking continued. She pushed a black dog back, and squeezed out the door, slamming it shut. "Sorry about that. We're just not used to visitors out here."

I smiled. "I bet. I hate to bother you, but we're investigators and we've been looking for a client, Billy Matlin, who disappeared recently."

"I think my husband told me about that. He might know him more than me. He's not home right now."

"Actually, we had hoped to hear more about your encounter with—"

There just wasn't an easy way to ask this, but luckily Eleanor piped up. "Is it true you faced down a beast out here on your property?"

She fumbled with the fabric of her dress. "Oh, well, my husband would rather forget about the whole thing, so it might be better if I don't talk about it."

"Is that what he told you to do?"

"Y-Yes, I think he's afraid someone might get a mind to have me committed to an institution."

"Easy for someone else to say you're crazy. Personally, I think unless you see something first hand, it just defies belief."

"Exactly. I'm alone out here a lot. My husband works in West Branch and commutes there daily."

"Oh, you poor dear," Eleanor said. "And here you're home with your children until the late hours of the night, I suppose."

"Yes, that's why I bought a dog. He makes me feel safe. Ever since I saw that thing staring at me through the window, I've been so afraid to be alone with the children out here."

"I don't blame you. So that's when you bought the dog?"

"Yes. My husband would rather I not call Sheriff Peterson back out here. I believe the man thinks I've lost my mind."

"Did he tell you that?"

"Not in so many words, but I could tell by the look on his face that he didn't want to believe my story. He kept insisting it was just a hunter walking across our property."

"Is that what really happened?"

"Not at all," she insisted. "I heard this awful noise like something was trying to get in the house. I dialed 911 right away. I felt drawn to the window in the kitchen, and that's when I saw it."

"What did it look like?"

She pressed a trembling hand against her chest. "It was a furry beast that stood at least six foot. He was sort of hunched over, but he stared right at me! I about had a heart attack on the spot."

"So what did you do?" I asked, taking in her account.

"I ran up the stairs and checked on the children, but luckily they were still asleep. I didn't come back down until I heard the rap at my door and saw the flashers from the sheriff's cruiser. Ten minutes later, my husband came home. Scott was quite upset about me calling the cops, but he just doesn't understand. I don't think he believed me at first either."

"Did the sheriff search your property to at least see if something was lurking around?"

"Yes, he had the deputies take spotlights and do a search, but they didn't find anything. It took me hours to get to sleep after they left and I was mad that Scott didn't believe me, but that sure changed the next morning. He was out in the lean-to. He was going to get some Tim Horton's donuts to make up for how he treated me the night before." She paused before continuing, "He came running back in the house in a panic not long after he went out the door. I was in the kitchen when he came back in. He was quite frantic and told me that he saw a hairy beast run across the yard. I begged him to call the sheriff back out here, but he refused. He insisted that we take care of this ourselves."

"Oh, and how did he plan to do that?"

"Bought a dog, for one thing, a German Shepard mix. He's quite the watchdog, one of the reasons I kept him inside. He doesn't take to strangers."

"Is he okay to be with your children alone?"

"Oh, yes. Quite the baby around the family, but if he doesn't know you, you had better watch out."

"What else did your husband do?"

"He and his buddies went out into the woods and did a search. They never turned up anything except for an empty cabin in the woods with the strangest thing."

My ears were peeled to what she said next. She claimed the cabin had a room that had chains connected to the walls, like something had been chained up—something with brown hair they found stuck in the links of the chain.

"Can you give us the directions to where that cabin is?" I asked intent on checking this out myself.

"Sorry, but my Scott and his buddies burned the cabin to the ground."

"They're darn lucky they didn't start a wildfire."

"That's what I told them, but we haven't seen that beast since."

I tried to absorb her account. "Do you think it was Bigfoot?"

"Not sure, but I could show you something." She walked to the back door and showed me three long scratch marks in the door. "This is all the evidence I have."

"No footprints?"

"No, it was pretty dry when this happened."

"Is there anyone else who can substantiate—?"

"Aggie means did any of your neighbors have similar sightings?"

"I can't say, since my nearest neighbor is a mile away."

We thanked Shelly and left, turning around 'cause there was just no way I was ever gonna be able to back down that length of a driveway.

Chapter Seventeen

"Can we please have lunch now?" Eleanor whined.

I nodded and made my way into East Tawas. Instead of going to the Whitetail Cafe, I headed to the campground where Martha had been staying. I secretly hoped that Martha would be there so that I could get news about my great-grandbaby.

I pulled alongside the camper, and luckily Martha's station wagon was also here. I knocked on the thin metal door, which made a horrible racket. Martha opened the door and ushered us inside. "Andrea is back at home, finally," she informed us. She looked a complete wreck, with dark circles under her eyes.

"I'm so glad to hear that. I really want to run right over there, but I imagine Sophia and Bill are exhausted after this ordeal."

"I didn't mean to keep you away from the hospital, but I was just trying to do what was best for Sophia."

"Oh, so the elderly aren't barred from visiting patients after all?"

"Sorry. I think Sophia and Bill were taking on more than they could handle as it was."

"I get it. You wanted to play doting mother."

"Yes, is that so bad?"

"No. I'm glad that you and Sophia are much closer. I must admit that when you rolled into town originally I might have judged you unfairly."

"You think?" Eleanor said as she raided the refrigerator. "Is this turkey and cheese I see in here?"

I smoothed my shirt into place, unsure what to say.

"Let's just keep that in the past. I haven't always been a model mother or daughter, but I like to think that I've changed my wicked ways, sort of," she winked. "I decided that Joshua Crabtree isn't too young for me. It might be fun to date again, or at least until he goes off to college and I'm a distant memory."

"Oh, so by date you mean more than one night?"

"Yes, Mother. If the two of you can have fiancés, there might be hope for me, too."

Eleanor piled the items she found in the refrigerator on the counter. "I hope you have bread, and not the wheat kind."

Martha gave Eleanor the bread and we made sandwiches. As I held my sandwich, I asked, "Did you give up on the vegan thing?"

"I was never a vegetarian exactly, but I do try to watch what I eat, not like it's a crime. Besides, Joshua is more of a meat and potatoes man." Martha drank a healthy portion of milk and dabbed at her lips with a napkin. "So how is the Bigfoot thing going?"

"Great, but the Animal Channel is suing the Animal Network and halted production of the reality series for now, but Andrew's on the case."

Her brow shot up, "Oh, he's back in town?"

"Yes."

"And where has Mr. Wilson been hiding, Eleanor?"

"He's been helping his granddaughter make salsa."

"I'm not sure if I've met her. We'll have to plan a barbeque soon."

Eleanor nodded. "Sounds like a plan, but we have so much to do yet. We still need to question Sheriff Peterson about the blood found at the Matlin place."

"And we also need to question the wildlife people," I added. "We haven't really caught a break just yet. I had hoped to find more clues before now. I think that reality show might be our best opportunity to do some real investigating, but with it shut down, I just don't know what else we can do."

"My sister, Margarita, is in town," Eleanor said. "It seems that she and her friends want to help with our investigation."

"Oh, you mean the girl that carries that bow around with her everywhere she goes?"

"Exactly," Eleanor said. "She's a little too pushy for my liking."

"She did say she's done some investigating in Bear Paw. She's just on the strong-willed side," I said. "We sent them on a wild goose chance out to the Matlin place to a Bigfoot sighting while we interviewed another witness."

"What did you make of it?" Martha asked. "Another basket case?"

"I'm not sure what to say about it. The lady sure seemed to be honest about what she saw. Not so sure about her story that her husband found a cabin in the woods where chains were affixed to a wall, or that he burned it down."

"You must be talking about Shelly and Scott Niles."

"So you've heard the stories before?"

"Sure, about a month back Scott was at Barnacle Bill's talking about that. Half of the patrons told him he'd better hush up before someone sent him to the loony bin, but a few locals said anything was believable in the area where he lives. That was way before everyone seemed hell bent on proving Bigfoot exists here in Tawas."

"Was that all that was said?"

"Yup, just Scott claiming to have burned out a cabin that might be the home to some beast. He never called it Bigfoot, but the descriptions seemed all the same to me. Now that I think about it, it was mighty strange that he never used that name. At first I thought he was thinking it was some sort of shapeshifter."

"Shapeshifter?" Eleanor asked. "What's that?"

"A person who can change from their human form to that of an animal, like a wolf or bear, really anything they want."

"Like a werewolf?" Eleanor asked interested.

"Except with a shape shifter, the moon isn't needed for them to shift. Some folklore claims they can shift at will. There is also many shifter romance books out there now, quite popular really. You should check out books about werebears."

Eleanor pulled out her iPhone and started an internet search and giggled. "Oh, wow. These books look really good. I should try one out."

"Check out the free ones. Many authors offer a first book in a series free. It's a way to check it out."

"That's fiction though, Eleanor. It won't help us investigate this case."

"No, but what if Bigfoot is really a shapeshifter? It might explain why he's never been found."

"I suppose it's all in what you want to believe. If you try to suggest that's the case, you'll be run out of town. Nobody has ever tried to say anything that ludicrous about Bigfoot before. The next thing you'll come up with is that Bigfoot is an alien."

Martha's face split into a grin. "That could be, too. The truth is that we just don't know if Bigfoot is real, or where he's come from. Like, how has he gone virtually undetected for all this time? With all the sightings, you'd think someone would have some kind of tangible proof by now."

"You do have a valid point, Martha, but that's what we're trying to figure out. When we're done eating, we'll head out to check on baby Andrea, and hopefully Bill might know where we can find the DNR and the Wildlife Service guys. I hope they're still in town, but I also hope that they test that hair we found at the Matlin place."

"What if it can't be determined? Where will you go then?"

"Somebody has to know something. We just have to find that someone who can help us solve this puzzle."

Eleanor and I finished our sandwiches and soon were heading down the road to Sophia and Bill's house. When I knocked on the door, Bill was dressed in his Michigan State Trooper blues. "Going back to work today?"

"I sure am. Andrea is doing much better, and Sophia is back to her old self. She's in the baby's room if you came to see her."

"Actually, we came here to see all of you. We've been quite busy with the Billy Matlin case."

He rocked back on his heels. "Oh? I thought you were looking for Bigfoot."

"You should know since Billy disappeared we'd be looking into where he might be. He can't pay us if he's not found, and since I don't believe Bigfoot swallowed him whole, we need to figure out where he is."

"Sounds like you have your hands full, but please be sure to relay any viable information to Sheriff Peterson or me. We're still investigating the matter."

"Great, so we're a team then?"

"I never said that. I still would rather have you two butt out. We both know that will never happen. Just don't put yourself into any dangerous situations." He raised both of his hands. "I know that's dang near impossible for the two of you."

My hands went to my hips. "Believe me it's not intentional by any means."

Eleanor fidgeted. "Have you heard anything about the blood found at Billy's, like did it belong to him or not?"

Bill sighed. "You know I can't tell you."

"Oh, you can tell them that at least, Bill," Sophia said as she strode into the room with baby Andrea squirming in her arms.

I walked over and took the baby from her. "Yes, the information is not that vital since I suspect the blood does belong to Billy. It was his house, after all."

"Since you already know, what are you asking me for?" With that he gave Sophia a peck on the mouth and was out the door.

Once the door slammed behind him, I said, "I just never know if that man is being sarcastic or if that was his way of telling me that I was right about the blood samples."

"Probably both, knowing my husband," Sophia said with a smile. "If you need to know, he barely talks shop at home. Probably too afraid I'd relay it to you, Grams."

"That's silly. You've never done anything like that, and I'd never put you in a situation like that. We always find our way to extract information. We'll be searching out Sheriff Peterson all the same."

"Why we gonna do that, Aggie? Trooper Sales already about told us that the blood was Billy's."

"True, but was that the only blood found? It seems to me that if something came flying through the patio door, it would be equally as injured."

"If you're assuming that it was an animal or beast like Bigfoot, and not an object like a brick or log."

"I don't recall seeing anything like that over at Billy's. Perhaps we should ask Margarita and company. After all, we sent them over there to check things out."

"Either you want them to help out with the investigation, or not," Eleanor sputtered. "Which is it?"

"Who?" Sophia asked.

"Margarita is Eleanor's sister, and she brought two gals to town with her that apparently helped solve a case back over in Bear Paw."

"Let me get this straight. Eleanor has a sister who has investigated a crime before too, but in another town?"

"From the sound of it," I acknowledged.

Sophia laughed for a moment. "Sorry, but that's just funny. Does Margarita also have a senior aged friend along for the ride?"

"Nope, a just a couple of gals originally from Louisiana. I never heard the story as to why they're still in Michigan."

"They're helping my sister with her restaurant. It seems they've converted her restaurant to serve Cajun cooking."

"Here in Michigan?"

"I love Cajun cooking," Sophia said as she pulled a filled bottle from the refrigerator, warming it under hot water that jutted from the sink spigot. "We should invite them over for dinner."

"I can't imagine we'd have much time for that unless the reality show really is put off indefinitely."

"True, and we can't very well invite her over and expect her to cook, but I hope at the very least that she could share some of her recipes."

"Sounds good, Sophia. I'll bring it up to them when I see them next." I handed the baby back to Sophia who was poised with the baby bottle. "We really should get going. We just wanted to stop by and check on you and the baby. I'm glad that you all seem fine now."

"It sure was quite the scare. Bill really proved to be a standup guy. You just never know what kind of father or husband a man will be. The pregnancy thing happened so quickly and so did our marriage. I was so worried that Bill might have felt pressured to marry me, but I can see now that was not the case. I know he loves me as I do him, and he's a great father. He did his turns at the hospital just like I did. One of the nurses even told me that he insisted on being very hands-on and wouldn't let them do much in the way of feeding or diaper changes. Tell me what kind of man does that?"

"One who loves you both with his whole heart," I said as I gave her shoulder a squeeze.

Eleanor and I left, confident that everything in this house was just as it should be. Baby Andrea showed no signs of illness now, and Sophia appeared quite rested.

Chapter Eighteen

When Eleanor and I waltzed into the sheriff's department we were led straight away to Sheriff Peterson's office. We walked in and he motioned us to two chairs as he was on the phone.

"I know, but I'm sure they weren't aware that they shouldn't be crossing the police tape. They don't live in East Tawas. They're from Bear Paw from what I saw when I looked them up on the computer."

Peterson locked eyes with me. "Not to worry, just let them go on about their way. I'll make sure that Agnes Barton explains to them how crime scenes work in Iosco County."

I gulped hard. "Uh-oh," Eleanor whispered. "No wonder we were led back here."

It could also be that most of the people at the sheriff's department know Eleanor and me quite well by now. We probably have a frequent flyer card. Not that we clock time here, but because we come here often enough to warrant an escort straight to the sheriff's office. Not all that long ago, Sheriff Peterson and I were practically at each other's throats, but we've grown accustomed to each other. He knows full well that we won't ever completely stay out of investigations, or what's left of his hair.

Peterson hung up his phone and asked us, "Would you two care for coffee?"

"You're offering?" I asked Peterson. "That would be great."

Instead of calling someone in to fetch it, he disappeared into the other room, returning with two cups filled with fragrant coffee. As we took the offered cups, I thanked him. "This sure is a switch. It makes me wonder what's up. I couldn't help but overhear part of your conversation."

"I bet not, but no worries there, except I had expected the two of you to be the ones over there to investigate. I had no idea that Eleanor's sister, Margarita, was in town, or that the two young ladies with her fancy themselves to be investigators. I heard they helped solve a case in Bear Paw."

"I don't know much about that case. They never went into elaborate details."

"That's surprising. So why did you send Margarita and company out there to the Matlin place?"

"They wanted to help, but Eleanor and I like to work a case between ourselves. You should know that by now, Clem."

He shifted his bulk on his chair that strained under his bulk. "Strange, Agnes, because Margarita mentioned that you told them to go out there to the Matlin place to check it out."

I cringed, but informed the sheriff, "Actually, I told Tammy Rodrigue they could help us out by checking to see if Billy had returned home, is all."

"So you think Billy would return home just like that after all the blood he lost?"

"Oh, I had no idea if all that blood belonged to Billy or not. So it was his blood, then?"

Peterson slapped his palms on his desk. "You know dang well it was."

I feigned innocence. "Oh, and how was I to know that for sure? It's not like I took DNA samples, or have a lab at my disposal."

"No, you don't, but I'm sure Trooper Sales already told you the blood was Billy's."

"Actually, Trooper Sales has been quite busy since his baby had been admitted to the hospital, and he doesn't bring his work home with him."

Peterson leaned back in his chair. "I'm sorry about your great-grandbaby, but I just would hate to see Bill get into any trouble by letting pertinent information slip into the wrong hands. I'm afraid you girls don't understand the importance of keeping this case out of public knowledge."

"That's where you're wrong, Sheriff. Did you find any other blood on the scene, besides Billy's?"

"You should know by now the chain of evidence doesn't drift down to the both of you."

"I know. I just wondered, is all. I just hope that you're not trying to hush up the Bigfoot stories. What if Bigfoot really is in Tawas?"

"He's not, trust me."

"Oh, and what about that time when you were called out to Scott and Shelly Niles's place?"

He gnashed his teeth together. "I don't know what you're talking about."

"Sure you do. You were called out to their place like a month ago, wasn't it? But according to Shelly, you didn't exactly buy into her story."

"Listen, we've been called out to many homes of area residents. We take all of their Bigfoot stories with a grain of salt. There is just no such a thing as Bigfoot. Billy Matlin has stirred the whole town up with his wild tales."

"Perhaps, but Shelly never said that it was Bigfoot on her property, just that something strange happened out at her place."

"Yeah," Eleanor said. "Something stared at her through her window. How can you discount that?"

"I'm not. We swept the property and turned up nothing. No footprints or signs of anything out of the ordinary."

"How about the scratches on the back door?"

"Anyone could have made them. It proves nothing."

"Did you hear the story about how Scott Niles supposedly burned down a cabin in the woods?"

"That's a new one. They certainly never shared a story like that. I would have taken action."

"Oh, so you can't really launch a Bigfoot investigation, but you can try to charge a man for arson of an abandoned cabin in the woods?"

"Look, there's nothing to substantiate Shelly's claims, and later I heard that the strange goings on had halted."

"So you can admit that there were strange goings on then?"

"I believe that Shelly believed it, but the truth is that she lives in a remote area and is alone while her husband works out of town. It's easy to conjure up these stories. Probably she was watching too many reality shows like the *Dead Files*."

"That show is about paranormal activity, like ghosts," I clarified.

Peterson swung his hands skyward. "I give up. There is just no pacifying you, is there, Agnes?"

"I'm not saying that. I was just questioning your reasoning about not believing Shelly's story."

"If I had seen something that I believed warranted a further investigation, I'd have done it. There just wasn't enough evidence. If you need to know, the Billy Matlin case is more worthy of an investigation."

"So, what is going on with that?"

"All the blood samples belonged to Billy. None of the dogs picked up much of a scent. They lost it at the river. Not much else to do. We could inform the public on this one, but the last thing I need to do is have more people tromping out in the woods."

"I see. Thanks for the share. I have no idea how we're going to find Billy, but I really believe that the reality show just might be the key."

"How so?"

"Well, for one it will give us a chance to search the woods more. I'm really interested to see what the Animal Network has in store for us."

"Like in—you're going to be on the show?"

"Yes, why?" Eleanor said. "We're old, not dead."

"Believe me, I know that more than anyone else in town. I have yet to call either of you out. I just hope that you'll both be very careful. I'd hate to have something happen to either of you."

Eleanor smiled. "Not to worry. We'll do just fine."

Sheriff Peterson glanced at his watch. "Thanks, ladies, but I have a meeting soon."

"What about the DNR and U.S. Fish and Game Service?"

"You'll have to catch up to them about the DNA samples. They're the ones responsible for that investigation. Personally, I believe those fellas are looking for more of a human connection to the crimes of killing that bald eagle. I sure hope that wasn't the same bald eagle carcass that I saw on US 23, but I suppose you two would know better than to plant roadkill as a potential crime scene just so you can get them to do a DNA analysis on that bunch of hair you found."

I blinked as I tasted bile at the back of my throat under his hard stare. "I hope you aren't expecting me to respond to that suggestion."

"Of course not. I know you value taxpayers' money more than that, and I'd hate to see either of you in trouble over the deal. You might want to tread lightly in the future."

Eleanor fidgeted. "We'll keep that in mind, but I didn't have anything to do with that bald eagle." I cleared my throat and El added, "I mean, we have no idea how that bald eagle was killed, but it's our hunch Bigfoot likes birds for dinner. Obviously, Billy didn't feed him enough to fill his stomach since he's so big."

I had to bite my lip to keep from laughing over El's weird assumption. "Do you happen to know where we might find the DNR this time of day?"

"Barnacle Bill's might be the place. I'm sure they're off duty by now."

I was thinking how the DNR sure didn't work all that hard, unless you count them asking for your fishing license to make sure you had one. I somehow envisioned them kicking back in that truck of theirs playing games on their Smartphones, but then again, I can be a mite judgmental sometimes. Especially when they were so reluctant to test the animal hair we had.

"Come along, Eleanor. We better hurry if we hope to catch them before they leave town."

Once we were outside, Eleanor asked, "How does Sheriff Peterson know we planted that roadkill?"

"Shhh," I said as we passed a few deputies on the way to the car.

We tore out of the parking lot and I parallel parked on Newman Street shortly after, this time without running over the curb. When we walked across the street I saw the DNR officers, Derek and Patrick, seated on the patio that faced Newman.

We waltzed inside and sashayed past the bar full of happy twenty-something's, making our way onto the patio. Neither of the men glanced up as they were completely engrossed in their nacho supremes they were devouring.

"Ahem," I said to get their attention.

Patrick glanced up first, swiping at his mouth with the back of his arm. "I was wondering when you two planned to hunt us down."

Derek raised his glass filled with beer with plenty of head foamed to the top, which slipped out over the rim as he guzzled it. He set it down and informed us, "We don't have anything to share just yet."

"No? So you and Duane from the U.S. Fish and Game Service aren't finished arguing about the DNA evidence yet?" When Derek didn't answer, I had to ask, "So what gives, really?"

"Don't you dare, Patrick!" Derek reminded him.

"Don't he dare what?"

"Oh, it's just that Duane is dating Derek's ex-wife, Marion, and this whole deal hasn't gone according to plan. Duane is refusing to allow the test to happen until his boss comes back from the Midwest."

Derek slammed his fist on the table. "He's tying it up on purpose. Our boss was adamant about having the tests run by today, but that never happened."

"Well, who has custody of the evidence?"

"The fish and game people, like always. I'm so sick of getting trumped by them. It's bad enough that I lost my wife to one of them idiots."

"Now that's not totally true, Derek. Duane never started dating your ex until last week," he consoled his co-worker. "I'm sure this will be cleared up soon."

"Still, it's easy for you to say. When I went to pick up my son yesterday, that damn fool was playing ball with my kid."

"Well, maybe you oughta spend more time with your boy and less time saucing it up."

"It's so easy for someone to say that when they've never had a relationship with a woman their whole darn life, let alone know what it feels like to be ousted out of their own son's life by some infiltrator."

Patrick hung his head for a moment and when he raised it again, he shot back with, "You've had too much to drink already. You're a mean drunk, Derek." Patrick smiled at us. "I've dated plenty of women. I guess I just never met the right one."

"You could stand to lose a few pounds, Patrick. You look like the Pillsbury dough boy."

"See? What did I tell you ladies? He's in a real mean mood tonight."

"I don't care to hear all of your personal business. We need a resolution to this case, which includes testing that evidence. Now Billy Matlin is missing. What if there was something in those samples that might just solve this mystery once and for all. And all of your bickering prevented Billy from being found?"

Derek rubbed his nose. "That's a good point. I'll use that tomorrow when we meet up with Duane to discuss the matter."

"Where is that gonna happen?"

"We can't tell you that. This is a private matter. Plus, you two fancy yourself investigators, which means we don't have anything more to say to you," Patrick said.

"Okay, but that is only one matter you should be trying to clear up. What about all the game hunters who have piled into East Tawas recently? Are you at least working with the fish and game people on that?"

"Yes, we're not idiots, you know. I can tolerate Duane to a point."

"Well, then, tolerate him enough to get that evidence tested, and soon."

"What are you doing about the game hunters?" Eleanor asked. "Yesterday they were carrying their firearms in plain sight."

"Sheriff Peterson and his deputies handed out citations to the offenders, and I believe that matter was taken care of."

"How are you planning to prevent them from going out into the woods and start blasting something?"

"We have more officers headed here tomorrow. We'll make sure that doesn't happen. We've been handing out fliers and a news story will be featured on the nightly news tonight."

"So where do you think Duane might be tonight? Perhaps if we speak to him, it might help out."

"Good luck with that one, but knock yourself out," Derek said as he guzzled more beer."

"I think you've had enough to drink, Derek. How about we run you home so you can sleep it off?"

"I'm doing just fine. I don't need no old bag telling me what to do."

Eleanor whipped the chair from underneath Derek's narrow behind and he fell to the floor with a very loud thump. "Dang it all. What did you do that for?"

"Divine intervention. Now come along and we'll take you home. No woman is worth drinking yourself half to death over," Eleanor said.

Derek was helped to his feet and he threw money down to pay his bill. We helped him back to our car. He stumbled all the way, muttering about how he wasn't too drunk to drive.

I opened the back door of the car, and he swung himself in like he was climbing into the Batmobile, thumping his head on the door. "Oww!" he cried.

Patrick climbed in the other side and said, "Thanks for the ride. Neither of us can afford a night in jail for drinking and driving." He proceeded to rattle off the address where they were staying, but it was no more than a hop and a skip from Newman Street as it was at the Tawas Bay Beach Resort which was ideally located right on the bay and in the same location that was where the tent campground had been quite some years back.

We dropped them at the door and they informed us they would be meeting Duane tomorrow morning at the sheriff's department. As they stumbled inside, I whirled away.

"I sure wish we could find Duane so we could straighten this matter up tonight."

"I know you do, Agnes, but it is best to wait until tomorrow. It would have worked better if both parties were together. Now you're gonna have to ask the same questions all over again."

I drove to Eleanor's house and noticed a beat up blue Impala in the driveway, minus the occupants. "Who's here, Eleanor?"

"Oh, it's probably Mr. Wilson and Millicent, his granddaughter. You might as well come in and say hello before you head out."

I nodded as I got out of the car, following Eleanor inside. "How did they get inside? Does Mr. Wilson have a key to your place?"

"No, but he sure has the key to my heart. You should know by now I always leave my doors unlocked."

"Oh? I could have sworn I locked them before we left."

Mr. Wilson pushed his roller walker toward Eleanor and gave her a peck on her cheek. "Hello, my sweet Eleanor. How I've missed you. I hope that friend of yours isn't getting you into too much trouble."

"Nope, we're both minding our manners these days, with the exception of Eleanor pulling out a chair from under a man at Barnacle Bill's."

"Sounds just like my Eleanor."

"I heard you two are looking for Bigfoot. How's that going?" Millicent asked as she popped the top of a soda.

I eyed Millicent's slight frame that was concealed beneath a sundress two sizes too big for her. "Just fine, but we haven't found Bigfoot yet. We're hoping that reality show, *Hunting Bigfoot*, will be able to shoot soon. Eleanor and I sure could use a break."

"Aren't you two afraid to meet up with a real Bigfoot out in the woods?"

"Yes and no, but honestly we haven't run into anything even close to a Bigfoot yet. So disappointing, really."

"Do you believe there is actually one roaming the woods of Tawas?"

"We've found some compelling evidence, but nothing conclusive just yet."

"I see. I'm sure you'll figure out something eventually. You always do."

"We always do," Eleanor clarified.

I took in a distinct aroma of fish and had to ask, "Is that tuna casserole I smell?"

"Sure is," Millicent said with a roll of her eyes. "You know how my grandpa is."

All too well, I thought. I wasn't so sure I could handle another portion of Mr. Wilson's famous tuna casserole. Not that it was bad. It was quite tasty until you had eaten it a few hundred times.

"It sure smells yummy, but I should head on home. My cat, Duchess, sure has a fit when I'm gone all day." This is not at all a lie.

I headed out the door and Eleanor told me she'd be ready by eight, hopefully plenty early enough to catch the wildlife guys at the sheriff's department in the morning.

On the way home, I kept my eyes peeled for anything strange enough to look like a Bigfoot crossing the road, but like always, I saw nothing. When I pulled in my driveway, Andrew's car was still parked here, but my lights were all on, so I assumed he must be inside. Sure enough, once I unlocked and opened the door, Andrew was waiting for me with a meowing Duchess in his arms. Once the door slammed shut, Duchess leapt from Andrew's arms and ran toward me. I leaned down and gave her a good petting.

"So Brent brought you back here?"

"Yes. I should have left with you. There wasn't much else I could do. The Animal Channel and the Animal Network have agreed to meet at the sheriff's department tomorrow morning to try to reach an agreement."

"Wow, the sheriff's department is going to be a hopping place tomorrow morning."

Andrew's brow furrowed. "I'm almost afraid to ask."

"It's just that the Department of Natural Resources and the U.S. Fish and Wildlife Service plan to meet there also."

"They still haven't analyzed the evidence they found out at the Matlin place?"

"Nope. It doesn't help matters that Duane from the wildlife service is dating the DNR guy's ex-wife."

"Still. They really need to get their act together. I'm glad I'll be there tomorrow. I wouldn't mind putting on some pressure."

"Oh? Like that's all it takes? It seems to be an internal conflict in their individual organizations."

"I have a good feeling that this will all be worked out tomorrow. We all need to move forward." He rubbed his neck. "Have you decided when you'd like to get married yet?"

Oh, my. Andrew had proposed to me some time back as did Mr. Wilson to Eleanor, but ever since then the subject hadn't been broached. Did I have nerve enough to go through with this? I fidgeted with my engagement ring. "I guess I've been too busy to think about setting a date."

"If you're not sure, then—"

"Why are you putting this on me? You no sooner proposed than you went back to Detroit for some legal case that you won't tell me anything about."

"As I recall, you and Eleanor left town for some investigating before I left for Detroit, and I'm not hiding anything. The legal things I do these days aren't important in the least. Unless you find wills and trusts interesting, but I do have a number of friends downstate that I socialize with."

"Where do you see yourself in five years? In Detroit or here with me?"

"Why do I have to choose? I don't see anything wrong with the way things are. We're both quite independent and are very involved in what we're doing."

"What about companionship?"

"We have plenty of that," he winked.

"Yes, when you're here we do, which hasn't been all that often of late."

Andrew reached to hug me, but I pushed him away. "Now is not the time. I'm too nerved up about what's going to happen tomorrow to think straight."

"Is that why we're fighting then?"

"I guess we haven't resolved our issues with each other. I love you, Andrew. I just can't think about marriage until we're on the same page."

"Which we won't ever be if we don't talk about it."

"I promise when this case is over—"

"When this case is over? It won't ever be the right time because just as soon as one case is solved, another pops up, demanding your attention. It's no wonder I go to Detroit so often." Andrew turned on his heels and went out the door, and with a scattering of stones he was gone.

Duchess looked up at me with knowing eyes. "I know, girl. I wonder if Andrew and I will ever see eye to eye about my investigating."

I batted at my eyes that began to burn a bit and I retrieved my eye drops, carefully adding a drop to each eye. At least now when my eyes teared up I could blame it on the drops and not how I felt at the moment.

When I finally was snuggled into bed, I couldn't help but wonder if Andrew and I would ever really walk down the aisle and get married. Perhaps I shouldn't have told him that I'd marry him in the first place.

I was on the verge of sleep when I heard a scratching noise at my window. I got up and hastily tied the rope of my robe around my waist, moving into the living room. Had I just imagined what I had heard? After standing in the nearly dark hallway that was lit only by a nightlight, I heard something scratching again, but this time on the front door.

I snuck up and moved my curtains aside slightly to see if there was something indeed out there. The motion detectors lights were on and I caught sight of something or someone dashing across my lawn, too fast to make out what it might be.

I stumbled over Duchess in search of my phone, and with shaking hands, dialed 911. I rattled off my address in a hurry, barely able to stop the pounding of my heart. "Calm down and tell me what you saw," the operator insisted. "I'm not sure, but I think Bigfoot is trying to get in my house."

"Bigfoot?" the operator laughed. "Is this a crank call?"

"Absolutely not! Are you gonna send the police out here or not?"

"Fine, I'll have them send out a squad car. Stay inside until they get there."

I hung up and dialed Andrew's number, blubbering to him about how I needed him. It must have been the sound of my voice because he didn't ask me any more questions. Just as Andrew hung up, bubble lights from two squad cars appeared as they entered my driveway.

I waited until I heard the rap at my door, and I opened it to Sheriff Peterson and Trooper Sales. I then told them what I had heard and that I thought Bigfoot was trying to get inside my house.

Sales raised a brow slightly as he jotted down what I had said. Lights again came in my drive. This time it was Andrew and I ran out to greet him. I threw myself into his arms and recounted to him what I had just told Sheriff Peterson and Trooper Sales.

When I pulled away, Andrew looked quite concerned as he guided me back inside and we sat down in the living room.

"Scratching at your windows and then your door?" Sales asked. "Did you look out the window?"

"Yes, and the security lights were on. I swear I saw something tall run across my lawn."

"How do you know it wasn't just a man who got lost and just happened to cross your property? There are plenty of strangers that have come to town."

"I know that! I tell you whatever it was, was hunched over slightly and quite tall."

"Are you sure it wasn't a bear?" Peterson asked.

"No, it wasn't a bear. I've had a black bear in my yard before and they don't move like that or walk around on two legs!"

Andrew rubbed my back. "Calm down, Aggie. It's going to be all right."

"Whatever it was scratched at my door and window." I got up and went to the door, opening it and fingered the grooves. "Look, there are scratches on my door."

Sales and Peterson examined the scratches. "Are you sure they weren't here before, Agnes?" Peterson asked.

"I'm positive. I'm old, not completely out of my mind, you know."

"No need to get upset, Agnes. I'm just trying to get a handle on what happened out here."

"Bigfoot tried to get into my house is what happened."

"If Bigfoot had wanted to get into your house, he would have," Sales said. "If it was really Bigfoot, I mean."

Sheriff Peterson gave Sales a narrow-eyed look. "Please tell me you don't believe that Bigfoot is roaming around in the woods."

"Of course not, unless that evidence found out at the Matlin place disputes your theory, Peterson."

My hands went to my hips. "What theory is that?"

Peterson sighed. "I'm not sure what really happened out there, but I can assure you that it wasn't related to Bigfoot."

"And you're basing that on what, common sense?"

"Exactly."

"You must have some theory about how the patio door was smashed in from the outside at the Matlin place, too."

"Billy might have staged it. Probably why we found his blood outside."

"Okay, then where is he now?"

"Dang it, Agnes. I don't know, but it just makes more sense."

"You're the sheriff though, and solving crimes is based on facts, not guesses—not even good ones."

"I came here to check out your property. I'll take my spotlight out there and have a look around." Sales followed the sheriff, and twenty minutes later they came back and announced that they'd be leaving.

I wandered back to my bedroom while Andrew locked up. Once he joined me, he said, "Promise me that we'll work on our differences. I love you and this relationship is important to me. We don't have to get married, but my proposal stands. Set a date if and only when you're ready. Agreed?"

"Agreed. Come to bed, Andrew."

Chapter Nineteen

At exactly eight o'clock in the morning, Andrew, Eleanor, and I were waiting in a conference room at the sheriff's department. Nancy, the clerk, came in and informed us that both the guys from both the Animal Channel and Animal Network would meet us at a conference room at the Days Inn.

I stood and asked, "What about the DNR and U.S. Fish and Wildlife Service?"

"They'll be meeting the sheriff at the Day's Inn, too, since he wants to be kept updated about what's going to happen with the reality show."

"I'm not sure why he's so concerned about that," I whispered to Andrew.

"He might have to have more deputies on hand, for security purposes."

We left for the Days Inn and were led into a conference room with the Animal Channel people and the Animal Network seated on opposite sides of the table. Eleanor and sat on a sofa close by, leaving Andrew to handle the meeting.

"I can imagine both parties would agree that a lengthy legal battle would be a strain on both the Animal Channel and the fledging Animal Network," Andrew began.

Chad smiled. "We would be happy to be a sponsor for the Animal Network, free of charge of course."

Peyton slammed his water glass down. "Free advertisement!"

"Unless you plan to tell the whole world that the Animal Channel inspired you to develop your own Bigfoot show."

"I'd rather say that than give you free advertisement."

Pierre DePaul stood up at the other end of the table. "So, it's agreed then. Peyton will release a press statement listing the Animal Channel as the inspiration of *Hunting Bigfoot*, and you'll drop your frivolous lawsuit."

"Not happening," Chad spat. "We want the advertisement."

"Isn't the Animal Channel a big dog as it is? Why would they need to be advertised on the Animal Network?" Andrew asked.

"They stole our idea," Chad said.

"It's loosely based, and these days it's hard to be that original. I'm sure you're not the only channel to think searching for Bigfoot was a good idea. Perhaps you stole the idea from someone on YouTube since there are tons of videos doing the same thing as you, Chad," Andrew insisted. "I don't think you want the public to think of the Animal Channel as bullies, which is exactly how I plan to spin it."

Chad leaned back in his chair as Pierre nodded and added, "No reason to swallow sour grapes here. We both can get along just fine. Our show isn't about experts analyzing Bigfoot claims. We're simply taking in a few groups to hunt for Bigfoot with the ultimate prize of ten million dollars. We'd be happy to donate one percent of our sales to an animal related charity of the Animal Channel's choice if we find proof that Bigfoot really exists."

"Aren't you the famous oceanographer Pierre DePaul?" Mike asked, obviously star struck.

Pierre nodded. "I'm also a filmmaker and conservationist."

"I've heard you've been likened to Jacques Cousteau."

Pierre shuffled the pile of paperwork in front of him. "I'm honored, but I'm not even in Jacques' league. Although I must say that he's a huge inspiration to me. I would have done just about anything to explore with him, but alas, I'm way too young for it to ever have been a reality for me."

Mike licked his lips. "Would you consider being interviewed by the Animal Channel? That way it would be clear that the Animal Channel holds no animosity toward you or the Animal Network."

"I think that's going too far now," Brent spouted off.

"Oui," Pierre said. "If it will help cinch this deal, I'd be more than happy to accommodate you since you lost out on interviewing Billy Matlin."

Andrew stood. "So are we in agreement?"

All heads nodded, including the Animal Channel's attorney who hadn't uttered a word. "I'll draw up the papers in the other room," Andrew said, disappearing into the next room.

"Thanks, Chad," I said as I made my way to the table.

Chad took a drink of water and then said, "Good luck, and you're all going to need it."

"I suppose you boys will leave right after you sign the papers," I said.

Chad stared me down and said, "After interviewing Pierre, don't you mean?"

"Of course, that's exactly what I meant."

Andrew was whistling as he came back into the room and pointed out where the Animal Network people, Brent, Peyton, and Pierre had to sign. Next, having the guys for the Animal Channel, Mike and Chad sign on the line. Andrew then pulled out a stamp from his pocket and stamped the documents, finishing up with his signature. "I'm a notary," Andrew explained.

After the Animal Channel people left the room, Peyton told Eleanor and me that they'd begin the show in a few hours, which would leave me plenty of time to deal with the wildlife people. Andrew left with Pierre, Peyton, and Brent to file the paperwork just as Sheriff Peterson and Trooper Sales entered the room. A server dressed in black trousers and a white button up shirt cleared the glassware and changed the tablecloth, then darted back out of the room, giving us plenty of privacy.

Both Peterson and Sales wore mirrored sunglasses like those television cops did years ago. Both men dropped their bodies into chairs, and only then did Peterson remove his eyewear. His squinty eyes looked bloodshot, and he had huge dark circles beneath them.

Sales pushed his sunglasses to the top of his head, and his eyes looked equally as appalling. "What happened to you two?" I asked.

Peterson swept a hand over his brow, removing the beads of sweat that appeared. "Well, after we left your place last night, Agnes—"

"Why were they at your house last night, Aggie?" Eleanor asked. "You never mentioned anything about that this morning."

"We didn't have time to go into all that." I then went on to tell her how I thought Bigfoot had been at my house and how it all played out by me calling 911.

"I just knew Bigfoot would come after one of us. I'm just glad it was you and not me," Eleanor said.

"It seems there was a run of Bigfoot sightings last night," Sheriff Peterson said. "Ten, to be exact, and Sales and I went on every call. I knew this would get out of hand, but I had no idea it would get this much out of hand. I haven't even been to bed yet."

"Well, hopefully you can sleep after the meeting with the wildlife people."

"What happened with the reality show? Did the two sides come to an agreement?"

"Yes, the show will begin in a few hours."

Peterson slammed his fist on his leg. "It figures. I'll have to make some calls to get in more deputies. You better do the same, Sales."

"Why do you need that many cops in town?" I asked.

"For one, we just don't know what's going to happen with that show going on and all the big game hunters in town."

"But didn't you handle that situation?"

"Yes, but I just know when that show starts taping, they'll all be heading into the woods, creating a huge problem for us."

The server brought in fresh ice water in a glass pitcher and glassware, leaving just as Derek and Patrick from the DNR entered, both with a manila folder clutched in their hands. Both men also looked out of sorts, with Derek looking the worst of the two. He was a shade of green that I haven't seen in quite some time.

"Good morning, Derek and Patrick."

"What's good about it?" asked Derek.

Trooper Sales arched his brow, "Am I missing something?"

"Nothing worth mentioning," I said. I had really hoped we wouldn't have to go all into that whole deal about Duane dating Derek's ex, but Derek was obviously still smarting over the matter. "Let's just focus on the matter at hand."

We all sat, waiting on Duane from the U.S. Fish and Wildlife Service who strolled in five minutes later. Behind him was a young woman with curly brown hair. Since they wore matching khaki pants and shirts, I figured they both worked for the wildlife service.

Duane introduced the woman, Bernadette Huntington, as his superior in charge of the investigation. "If I worked for someone that looked like you, I'd never be able to think straight," Derek said with a wink.

"Oh, really? And here I was thinking you'd be making fun of that awful last name of mine."

"Huntington is a real nice last name. It sounds very dignified, like you come from money."

"Exactly. My father is Senator Huntington. I've been trying most of my life to create my own identity. After all, I'm nothing like my father, but I guess the conservationist part is about the only thing we do have in common. He would rather I take a Washington job working for the Environmental Protection Agency. What a bore."

Derek couldn't seem to quit smiling at Bernadette, and I wanted to give him a kick under the table, but perhaps it might help him stay on task and forget all about Duane dating his ex-wife.

"Nice to meet you, Bernadette. I'm Agnes Barton and this is my partner, Eleanor Mason. We were the ones who pointed Duane to the bald eagle carcass we found on the Matlin's property. I'm not sure if you're aware, but Billy Matlin has since disappeared. That's why we think it's imperative for the evidence to be processed."

"Oh, my. I hadn't heard. I suppose that makes it impossible now to question him."

"Oh? I had thought that he was already questioned?"

"He was," Duane said. "We do like to do a follow up interview to make sure we have all of the facts."

"All I can see that needs to happen is to do a DNA analysis of what you found, like that brown hair."

"How do you know what we retained as evidence?" Duane asked.

"I couldn't help but notice brown hair near the crime scene. How are you going to be sure what animal might have killed the eagle if you don't analyze everything you found?"

"There wasn't much left of the carcass as it was, and I didn't notice any animal scat nearby that would help us determine what animal might be responsible, but we don't believe that a human was responsible."

"Then what is the hold up with the analysis?"

"We've been wrangling with the DNR over the chain of evidence."

"The U.S. Wildlife trumps the DNA," Bernadette said. "Sorry, boys," she said sweetly.

"That's fine. After all, our boss clarified that today. How about a consolation dinner?" Derek asked.

She smiled. "Oh, why not. I live dangerously, but I expect a home cooked meal. Are you up to that?"

"Sure, if you don't mind coming to West Branch where I live."

While we all stared wide-eyed, numbers were exchanged and now Duane was the one who looked green when Bernadette told him to get the evidence tested right away, escorting him out.

I was impressed. "Wow, Derek. You're a real player."

"Can't blame a guy. Did you see her? What a knockout."

"Just cool it on the sauce from now on."

"I will. It seems that Duane only went out with my ex the one time."

"But I thought he was playing ball with your kid."

"He was, but he was just trying to warm up to my kid while my ex was getting ready. That kind of stuff works with single mothers.

Marion didn't fall for it one bit. She thought Duane was a little full of himself, too."

"Oh? Did she tell you that?"

"Actually, yes. I left a drunken message on her answering machine and she called me back this morning. We got it all straightened out."

"That's not how you acted when you got here."

"What man wouldn't be pissed that the same man, who was already under my skin, dated my ex?"

"It's not something to get riled up about now, it's just life. Good luck with your date."

I stared at Peterson until he said, "Well, I guess I wasn't needed to moderate after all. Thanks, Agnes, and good luck with the reality show."

I marched out the door, confident past belief. I was more than excited to be finally competing on the reality show, *Hunting Bigfoot*. I made the two trips to both Eleanor's house and mine to change clothing, and once we were dressed in camouflage, we were soon roaring up the Cat Lady's driveway that was already filling with cars. Andrew was obviously too busy with filing the paperwork to make an appearance, which I was happy about. Eleanor and I preferred to work alone.

We sauntered up the few steps that led to the porch, and the Cat Lady, Bernice, opened the door. "Isn't this exciting?"

Eleanor and I were each given a number that was stuck to our backs. I had number 522 and Eleanor had number 677. Obviously they weren't using numbers in sequential order.

Margarita sat in the corner, nursing a coffee between her shaking hands. "Hello, there," I said. "Where is your number?"

"Oh, I'm not competing. I'm much too old for that."

I wasn't sure if she meant anything by that or not, so I ignored what she said. Tammy Rodrigue and her friend, Dixie, were chatting it up with Curt and Cutis Hill. Tammy had a pink bow in her hand, quite the difference to Curt's camouflage one.

I walked up to Tammy. "I have been wanting to talk to you about the little trip you took for us."

Tammy pulled her red hair back into a secure ponytail. "You mean the one that almost landed us in jail? Thanks for that."

I was about to apologize when Brent appeared and told us to file outside. Once we were all outside, he said, "I'd like to ask all of you to leave all your firearms behind. It's going to be difficult enough out here without worrying about one of you shooting me in the back." I didn't have a gun, but Eleanor offered up her pink pistol. I stared at the pile of firepower and thought it was a wise choice, but I had a sneaking suspicion that the Hill boys might not have come completely clean with their weapons, but I wasn't about to tackle that issue with either of them.

"The bows, too," Brent added.

Tammy clutched hers tight. "There is no way I'm giving up my bow. What if we run into a bear out there? Think, man."

Brent strutted over. "Don't worry. I'll protect you, babe."

"Babe?" Tammy gasped. "I don't see no damn babe out here. If you get out of line with me, I'm gonna put a real hurting on you."

Brent trembled. "I love a woman who's in control, if you catch my drift." He did move away from Tammy, though. "You'll all have to get used to cameras trained on you, and expect for them to get right up close to you. There are also boom microphones. We'll be taping everything you say to one another. You'll all be given a battery pack and a microphone piece that connects to your shirts."

I almost giggled when Bernice helped Brent's crew secure the battery packs around our waists. I ended up working the cords under my clothing, but Eleanor let one of the young men do hers.

Once we were all properly equipped, we were divided into our teams. On ours were the Hill brothers, and Tammy and Dixie. Tammy still had her bow, but Curt gave his up. Brent told us that he wasn't worried about a girl with a bow, suggesting that women simply weren't strong enough to do him any real damage. From the way Tammy gnashed her teeth together, he had better tread lightly with her. I really did believe that she might just do him harm.

The other team left and we were instructed not to leave for twenty minutes. Curt and Curtis carried most of the gear for our team because there was just no way Eleanor or I could carry more than a small bag of essential supplies, like an emergency supply of food that might get us through if we got ourselves lost in the woods. Plus, I knew Eleanor had her cell phone shoved down her bra. Eleanor was in charge of carrying the trail map.

Curt tried to lead the way, but Tammy sidled up next to him. That Tammy just couldn't have any man taking charge, it seemed. I kind of admired her, but there were times when it wouldn't hurt for a man to lead the way, like if there was a bear ahead of us on the trail.

Eleanor rattled off directions, but Curt all but ignored her. "Not to worry, Miss Eleanor," Curt said respectfully. "I know these trails like the back of my hand."

"Yes, but Brent told us which trail to follow," I said.

Curt stopped and turned to face us. "Do you want to really hunt Bigfoot or just play into the hands of those wannabe's? I'm sure we could all agree that Brent is a buffoon. Stick with me, and we'll be all splitting that ten million dollar prize money."

We all nodded in agreement, and I tried not to shake as birds took to flight, scattering leaves as they did, cascading down us like snowflakes. Maple and elm trees canopied us from high above, as there were no white pines yet in this area. The leaves were moist beneath our feet and I took in the scent of mustiness.

Branches cracked as we stepped on them, and Curt quickly snapped out orders not to be so noisy. He was taking this seriously. I swept my eyes from side to side, half expecting Bigfoot to show up at any turn in the trail, but so far nothing. After what seemed to be hours, we cleared the heavy brush and approached the abandoned hunting camp where we set up camp. There were a few cabins, but for the most part only wooded platforms that were two foot off the ground were there that I assumed would be good to put a sleeping bag on to sleep. They were certainly long enough for someone to lie on, but without a bit of cushion.

"In here, Agnes and Eleanor," Brent motioned to a cabin. "Peyton hauled down a few air mattresses here so that you wouldn't be too uncomfortable."

That sure made me feel at ease. We helped make a fire and Curt and Curtis came back with a few dead squirrels. I cringed, but Curt reminded me we were on a real game hunt and we needed to eat like we were. He made stew out of the squirrels, cooking them over an open fire in an iron pot that had been brought as part of our provisions.

The other team came into camp and then asked, "How did you get here before us? We left first."

"I guess we're just the stronger team, is all. You better just leave right now. There's no way you're fit to hunt Bigfoot. He was spotted last night, you know." All eyes were on me as I recounted the story about what happened to me last night.

"Weren't you scared?" Dixie asked with wide eyes as she leaned on Curtis's shoulder.

"I sure was, but the thing is, I just wasn't all that sure what I did see. The sheriff told us that a total of ten people claimed to be visited by Bigfoot just last night."

Everyone began to murmur amongst themselves. "Strange that we haven't seen any signs of him yet," one man said.

I shuddered at the thought. It was almost like a bad omen. I couldn't help but notice that Brent currently wasn't anywhere to be seen now, so I used this opportunity to speak with Tammy and Dixie, pulling them aside. As we moved between the cabins, I asked them what had happened when they checked out Billy Matlin's place—after we had disconnected our microphones, that is.

"Well, we crossed the police tape for one," Dixie began.

"I figured that much. Please, go on. What did you see on the patio?"

"What are you asking, exactly?" Tammy asked.

"Was there anything close by that might have been used to smash the window?"

"Sure. There was firewood out there, but nothing that looked big enough to do that kind of damage. We found a few broken pieces of bricks, too, but I can't say there was anything that could have done the job. Do you think Billy staged it?"

"That's certainly a theory, and his blood was on the patio, but that might have happened in a struggle. I guess I just wished there was something more."

"Not animal scat, either?" Eleanor asked.

"Nope. If that had been there earlier I'm sure it would have been taken as evidence, though," Tammy pointed out.

"One more question. How long were you there before the cops showed up?"

"Not long, huh, Tammy?"

"Nope, not long at all. The cops might not have finished with the crime scene or that's what they told us when they threatened to arrest us. We had to tell the cops you sent us there. I didn't want to spend the night in jail."

"I can't blame you, Tammy. Thanks for your trouble just the same."

"You never expected us to find any real evidence, did you?"

"Actually, no. We mostly just wanted you out of our hair so we could check out another lead, but so far nothing we've done has panned out."

"Keep the faith, Agnes. We might just run across a lead right here on this Bigfoot hunt."

We reattached our microphones and wandered back to camp. Brent was here now, standing near the fire, and from the look in his eye, I think he suspected that we had unplugged our equipment. I had no idea how that might have worked. Was it possible that they had some kind of computer network that was tracking our every move?

Brent crossed the distance between us in five easy strides. In his hand he held a box of some sort. He showed it to us and pointed out the map with four flashing circles that I assumed indicated an interruption of connection with our microphones. "The four of you disappeared from my grid for five minutes."

"Well," I began. "We must have walked into a black hole."

"The contract you signed states that you're not allowed to disconnect the microphone or any other pieces of the equipment attached to you."

Curt and Curtis bounded over. "Oh, great. I told Curtis that this was a bad idea. We could have just found Bigfoot all on our own."

"That only applies to contestants on this reality show. Now if you two would like to leave, that's just fine. I'll have one of the crew escort you back."

Curt took ahold of Brent's shirt and said, "We'll leave when we're good and ready and not before, and my brother and I certainly don't need anyone showing us the way home. We know these woods better than any of you."

"Calm down, Curt. This was all just a misunderstanding," I said.

When Curt let Brent go, he insisted, "I want the both of you off this reality show. Now!"

Two bald men came forward and stared down Curt and Curtis. I couldn't help but notice Curt's hand grabbed something from the back of his pants. "Please, can't we work something out here?" I said. "There's no need for violence."

Tammy nudged Curt in the side. "I'll meet you for drinks when this is all over."

Curt smiled widely and yanked the battery pack and microphone attached to him off with a jerk. "Fine by me, but there's no way any of you will find Bigfoot by being led around the woods by these yahoos."

Curtis began to nod his head. "Yeah, my brother's right. It was beginning to weird me out wearing this equipment, anyway. I was starting to think you're really working for the National Security Agency, Brent."

The Hill boys strutted out of the campsite and I had mixed feelings about it. I kinda felt safer with them around, and knew they at least had a concealed weapon somewhere that might prove handy in a pinch.

"Now what?" I asked Brent. "Do you want us to leave, too?"

"I can't afford to lose any more contestants, but boy was that some good drama for the show."

Peyton made his way toward us. "Brent, you need to cool your jets. Those boys made for some good television. Now all we have left is a couple of old ladies," he motioned toward Tammy and Dixie, and added, "and these two gals."

"What about the other team?" As I glanced around I didn't see them.

"They're securing the perimeter," Brent said.

I swatted at a mosquito. "What on earth for?"

"We don't want to be caught unaware if Bigfoot happens upon this camp. I've been told by the locals that this area has been active with sightings."

"Lucky for me, I have my trusty bow," Tammy said. "I'm a pretty good shot with this thing, even if I am only a girl."

"Please, don't do that. I don't want to worry about a lawsuit if you accidently impale anyone."

Her eyes narrowed to slits. "Oh, I think you're covered with that liability agreement you had us all sign."

"How about handing the bow over?"

"How about I don't shoot you with it? Will that do?"

Peyton just shook his head and walked away. I smiled. "Well, I guess that settles it then."

Chapter Twenty

The other team that consisted of four men sat across from us, moving the squirrel stew around their plates with disinterest. Tammy passed her own blend of seasoning our way, claiming it would make the stew twice as tasty.

I was unsure, but Eleanor and I used the seasoning all the same. I breathed in the now spiced food with interest. It didn't smell half bad. I didn't know all that much about Cajun cooking, all I did know was that it was on the spicy side.

Eleanor fanned her mouth after a spoonful. "This meat is a little grisly, but with these spices I can hardly tell what it tastes like."

"That's the beauty of my special spices," Tammy said. "I never leave home without them."

"I'm not eating this shit," one man spat, tossing it into the fire, spraying us with sparks.

"You idiot. You trying to catch us on fire?" I bellowed.

"Why are you old folks even out here? It's not like you're gonna find Bigfoot. I am."

"Oh, really? And what makes you so darn able?"

"The name's Barney Truffle. I hail from Alpena and I've been an outdoorsman for my whole life. I've hunted bear, wolves, cougars, white-tailed deer, and rabbits."

"Really? Strange, since two of those animals are on the endangered species list."

"No they're not. In the Upper Peninsula, you can hunt wolves from November 15th until December 31st or until the quota is met. According to the DNR, cougars don't exist in Michigan."

"I know all about that, but we both know that isn't true."

"Well, I killed a few out west when I visited my brother. They were causing problems with his livestock."

"I see. What's the story with the rest of you?"

Robert Greer, Ivan Bauer, and Terry Jasman also introduced themselves, each of them with hunting backgrounds. Stiff competition, to be sure.

Tammy and Dixie went back with us to our cabin. I insisted that they stay in there with us for safety's sake. Eleanor and I climbed on the mattresses that sat atop the wooded platforms and I groaned at how uncomfortable it was. I just hoped Eleanor fared much better.

"How you doing over there, Eleanor?"

"I'm gonna have a backache when I wake up."

"Me too, but let's try to get some sleep."

Tammy and Dixie were asleep faster than I would have thought possible. I was like that when I was younger, too."

Howls were heard in the distance, and my only hope was that the coyotes stayed far from camp. The glow from the fire could be seen through the window and that gave me some comfort. That should keep wild animals away, but I wasn't so sure about Bigfoot, he sure never stayed away from my house last night.

I closed my eyes with the intention of going to sleep, but my mind just wouldn't. I heard voices right outside our window. "This oughta scare them but good," a male voice said. Scratches were then heard with groans and growls that didn't sound a bit animal-like.

I ignored the noises and obviously nobody else heard them, and Eleanor was snoring. I sighed, and that's when it hit me—that foul odor that Eleanor and I had first smelled back at Billy Matlin's place. I grabbed my blanket tight when I heard an awful commotion outside, loud footsteps, whooping noises, and blood curdling screams.

"What the hell?" Tammy said, as she leapt to her feet with bow in hand, pulling an arrow from her quiver, readying her bow for action.

"One of the guys out there must be just messing around."

"It sure smells bad out there," Dixie said, her voice quivering.

Eleanor somehow was still snoring away like nothing was happening. I rolled off the mattress and crept closer to the door, chancing a look out. The camp was completely empty, the fire no more than embers.

"What should we do?" I asked Tammy.

"Why you asking me? You're the big time investigator."

"Yeah, for criminals, not a huge hairy beast."

"Maybe we should go outside and take a look around," Dixie suggested.

I gave her a look, but in the darkness it lost its power. "You can go ahead, but I'm staying right here, unless—"

"Unless Bigfoot decides to come in here?" Dixie finished for me.

"That's not what I wanted to hear."

"Well, what you want to hear and what you're gonna hear are two different things," Dixie said.

"Would you both hush," Tammy whispered. "I'd rather not meet Bigfoot tonight."

"Why are you here then?"

"Oh, I don't know. I just planned to take a few pictures from a distance. Like a far distance away."

"And here I figured you for the brave one."

"We're all closed in here. If Bigfoot decides to check out the cabin, all I'll have the chance to do is shoot one arrow."

"Oh, some archery champ you are."

"I'm used to shooting at targets, not a ferocious beast intent to gobble me up."

"Don't be so melodramatic. Plus, I think he's gone now. I don't hear anything."

"How are you supposed to with the way you keep yapping?"

Instead of giving Tammy a curt reply, I peeled my ears to determine if what had been outside was still there, or long gone now. I crept over to the window and all I could see was—nothing. I heard something large tossed around outside, and Tammy and Dixie huddled with me. "It's definitely out there still," Tammy whispered to me.

The smell came closer, and we kept ducked down just as something walked toward us with a series of thumps. My hair moved as a rush of hot and foul breath came through the window that had no glass. I trembled, my heart now thumping like a drum. Bigfoot was standing just outside.

Eleanor's snores ceased, and I held my breath, praying that she wouldn't freak out now. When I heard a thump, I figured it was Eleanor as she crawled to us. She hugged me tight, shuddering. My knees shook now and hurt so bad that I collapsed onto the floor. Luckily, I was cautious when I did it, not making a sound.

Footsteps moved away from us now, taking the foul air with it.

What should we do now?" Eleanor asked. "Sounds like he's gone."

"We need to stay here," I recommended. "It's too dark outside to see anything and I'm certainly not risking meeting up with Bigfoot in the dark."

"Or at all," Tammy said. "I don't even date hairy men."

🐾 🐾 🐾

We waited until the first rays of daylight came from the east. Eleanor was as sore and achy as I was and Tammy and Dixie wanted to go back to Louisiana where the worst they had to worry about were alligators. They knew how to deal with them … stay far away, or carefully capture them.

When we finally left the cabin, the camp was in complete disarray. Cameras, tripods, and boom microphones were smashed on the ground.

"Let's take a look around and see if anyone else is here," I suggested.

We looked in the other cabin, but it was empty. "It looks like everyone is long gone," Tammy observed. "What do you suggest we do now?"

"Look for the survivors."

"Look where?" Dixie asked.

"We'll have to get deeper into the woods, I suppose. We just can't leave without at least trying to find the men."

Tammy massaged her chin. "What was it that Peyton said; the only people left are old women and girls? Looks like girls rule to me."

"I'm glad you're on board. We might as well head out."

We searched the campsite and found meager supplies, like snack cakes in Brent's cabin, which we completely devoured.

"I spoke into the microphone. "I'm not sure if this is working or not, but we're the lone survivors of this hunting party. I'm not sure what happened last night. All I know is that all of the men have disappeared, leaving two old ladies and two girls from Louisiana to find the men folk. Send help if you hear this transmission."

"You're funny," Dixie said, with frosting dripping from her lips from a Little Debbie snack cake.

We made our way back onto a trail that we decided to take based on footprints leaving the area. Eleanor was in charge of the map, which was great since we didn't want to get completely lost.

We hadn't made it far on the trail before white pines overtook the landscape.

"It's beautiful out here," Dixie sighed. "And the air is so crisp smelling."

"That's Michigan for you, and as you can see it's quite misty out yet." And it really was, hovering near our feet as we followed the trail.

The trail we were on began to get mushy.

I saw wetlands in the distance, but off to the left there was a cabin that looked to be abandoned. I made my way over there and I tried the door, but it was locked. Tammy took a hold of the doorknob and rattled it something fierce. The handle came off in her hands. She then began to shoulder the door open with Dixie's help. It slammed against the opposite wall and I pressed my arm against my nose from the foul odor that emitted from within.

"Should we go in, or—?" I hesitated, "—Eleanor, do you still have your cell phone on you?"

She reached into her cleavage and retrieved it, trying to make a call. "Hello, we need help out here." Eleanor pulled her phone from her ear. "It went dead."

"Who did you call?"

"I don't know if I called anyone."

"Well, check would you? It might be the difference between life and death."

Tammy walked into the cabin. "Place looks empty."

Dixie pointed out a trap door on the floor. "What about down there?"

Between Tammy and Dixie, they managed to get the door open. "There's a ladder down there," Dixie said. "I'm not sure if we should check it out."

"How else are we gonna figure out what's happening?"

Tammy and Dixie played rock, paper, scissors with their hands and fingers, to decide who would go first. "Scissors cuts paper," Dixie said. "Tammy, you're first."

Tammy went down the stairs, but came back within minutes, pale as a ghost. "We'd better get out of here before—"

"What's down there?" I interjected.

"I'm not sure who it is, but he's quite dead."

"Oh, to hell with it. I'll have to go down there and check myself." I had to know if it was anyone I knew.

"But, Agnes," Eleanor said. "You have a bad hip."

"I know that, but it's been much better of late. I'll just go down far enough to try to identify the body."

Tammy gave me a look of uncertainty. "Are you sure you should? Perhaps we should go get the cops and let them do the dirty work."

I ignored Tammy and descended the stairs. A man was secured to the wall with chains that cut into his arms and had a rope around his neck. He was slight in frame and I had to suck in a breath as I lifted his head. I then stared into the face of the very dead Billy

Matlin. I lowered his head again, and searched his body for other possible wounds, and finding none, determined that the he might have choked to death from the rope that was around his neck as it was tight enough to create quite a deep indent in Billy's neck.

I heard a few thumps from above, but figured it was the other girls. I glanced around, but there was nothing down here that would give me any indication of who was responsible for Billy's death. When I climbed back up the stairs, Tammy, Dixie and Eleanor were standing against the far wall with their hands held high in the air.

Brent stood there with a gun in his hand. He turned in my direction and motioned me toward the far wall where I joined my friends. "Why did you kill Billy?" I asked.

"He was getting in my way. How was I supposed to do a show about hunting Bigfoot if he found him first?"

"You must have figured out that one of us would run across Billy's body during this show. Seems to me that you would have gotten rid of the body at least."

"Actually, I didn't plan for us to even take this trail."

I felt Tammy's body stiffen, but her bow was clear across the room where she had set it down before she descended the ladder and found Billy's body.

"How did you kill Billy, though? I didn't see any visible wounds."

"It's all Peyton's doing. He tied that rope around Billy's neck and it somehow choked the poor fella, but it's just as well since there was just no way that I could let him go."

"Poor Billy. He didn't do anything to deserve dying that way, or any kind of way."

Brent shrugged. "I didn't have a choice."

"What do you plan to do with us now?"

Brent leered at Tammy. "Hey, girl. How do you like me now?"

"I'd like you dead, actually. Lucky for you that my bow is way across the room."

"It doesn't have to be this way, Tammy. We could have a little fun before I have to kill you."

"It would take more than a gun before I'd go along with that."

Brent rubbed his chin. "I really wish there could be another way, but you found Billy's body. If only you had stayed on the trail. We had planned to have a great show. Agnes's last transmission back at the camp was priceless."

Brent made my skin crawl. "What do you plan to do to us?"

"Well, after what happened last night, I figure that we'll have to make it appear like Bigfoot ripped you from limb to limb."

"We'll drown them in the river," Peyton said as he walked into the room. We can't just cut them into pieces and make it look real. They'll do a DNA analysis and that won't ring true."

I must admit that I liked the drowning scenario much better than being ripped limb from limb. "Why not just let us go? We won't tell anyone about what happened here."

"Not happening," Peyton said. "Plus, after the other contestants recount their stories and the film footage of last night, Pierre will have to choke up the ten million dollars. It's in the contract that we'll be awarded twenty-five percent of the prize money. It just makes sense that Bigfoot did you in."

"So you plan for Bigfoot to take the blame here? How on earth do you plan to get the other contestants to go along with you?"

"Seventy-five percent is still quite a sum of money," Peyton said.

"But isn't your getting a portion of that money a conflict of interest?"

"Pierre arranged the show this way. We need our cut too for leading a bunch of inexperienced people into the woods to hunt for Bigfoot. Once this story hits the airwaves, we'll be famous. What other reality show can boast they found Bigfoot? Certainly not those fools from the Animal Channel."

"None of the other contestants were back at the camp. What do you plan to tell them, or are they in on your scheme, too?"

"No, but they certainly played into my hands last night."

"I didn't see any of them back at the camp. I bet they might right now be at the sheriff's department. I bet Sheriff Peterson is organizing a search party as we speak."

"Good try. The other contestants are still locked up below ground at the camp. I told them it was for their own safety, and that we were planning to call Sheriff Peterson to lend us a hand. We'll release them after you're disposed of."

"I suppose you think you're pretty smart, don't you?"

"What about what happened last night?" Tammy asked. "Did you stage that whole Bigfoot thing?"

"We had planned to, but I guess the real Bigfoot had other plans. The film footage was much better than we could have hoped for. Even our Bigfoot suit wasn't half as good as the real deal," Peyton went on to say.

"So you were the ones who were at my house?"

"Yes," Peyton said. "It was very believable, wasn't it?"

"And you did the same thing at other houses in the area, ten to be exact?"

"Yes, we had hoped that would create a buzz, but Sheriff Peterson obviously kept it under wraps. If only we had more time. I'm sure the residents would have started talking to the press."

"So you wanted to create more of a buzz for your show?" Eleanor asked.

"Exactly."

"I must congratulate you on your Bigfoot farce at my house. You sure made a believer out of me."

"We aim to please," Peyton said. "But enough talking. It's time to get moving."

We were led from the cabin and ushered toward the wetlands and the Au Sable River. Birds flapped their massive wings and rose to the air, while frogs croaked.

Eleanor and I held hands as we were heading toward our doom, our feet sinking to our ankles in the muck of the wetlands. After about five minutes, I heard the familiar whooping sound, but instead of being frightened, I felt calm. Was it too much to hope that Bigfoot would save the day and us? The further we walked, the more apprehensive I felt. Was this it for us? I wrinkled my nose as a stench wafted in the air, causing me to sneeze. I frantically glanced behind us, but so far no sign of Bigfoot. No sign of anything. Branches cracked beneath our feet as we continued toward the river, but the sound echoed like it wasn't just us making that noise, like something or someone was following us. Two Great Blue Herons from their nest high above our heads went into flight with a whirl of their massive wingspan, like something had spooked them. Three whitetail deer zigzagged ahead of us, too, making their way through the white pines. It was deadly quiet now, not one bird singing, no cricket chirping, nothing. Just then, the familiar whooping sound split the quiet of woods again, the same sound that Eleanor and I heard before.

"That sounds like Bigfoot," I said.

Tammy sneaked a peek behind her. "I think she's right. You might as well just let us go now. You don't want to make Bigfoot angry."

Brent snarled. "Keep moving, Red."

A chill crept up my spine as something quite large lumbered toward us, tree limbs snapped, and growls were heard, not to mention that God-awful stench.

Eleanor and I hugged each other tight, trembling.

"Get moving, grandmas, or I'll shoot you where you stand," Brent threatened.

"That would be hard to explain away, now wouldn't it? I can't imagine that Sheriff Peterson would buy that story. He knows us better—"

Peyton wrenched us apart and I screamed in pain. Something large and hairy came at us like a lumbering linebacker. Tammy pulled Eleanor and me with her, followed by a panicked Dixie. We waded through the marsh, hoping to put distance between us and Brent and Peyton who were now screaming like girls.

As we approached the edge of the mighty Au Sable, Curt and Curtis appeared from a clump of trees with rifles in their hands. Curt helped us conceal ourselves in the brush and placed a finger against his mouth in a shushing motion. He handed Tammy a pistol and disappeared, presumably to help his brother take on Brent and Peyton. I listened intently, but no shots were fired at first, but then two shots cracked off. I tried to catch my breath, unsure if we should move or stand our ground. The bushes ahead of us swayed and Tammy cracked off a shot that ricocheted off the trees.

"Watch out, little lady. You almost shot me," Curt said as he stumbled forward. "You won't believe what just happened."

My eyes widened as I asked, "What? Did Bigfoot get Brent and Peyton?"

"I'm not sure what happened, but they sure are shaken up."

"We heard a few shots. Curtis didn't shoot Brent and Peyton, did he?"

"Nope, Brent and Peyton said they tried to shoot Bigfoot, but missed. They gave up right away when they saw us, rambling on about how Bigfoot almost tore them limb from limb."

I laughed nervously now, and Curt helped us make it back onto the trail. We finally saw what Curt was talking about. Brent and Peyton were completely soaked in mud and smelled like they had peed themselves. I had to laugh about that after what they had intended to do to us.

"What happened to you two?"

"Bigfoot came at us is what. He knocked us down, and we landed in the mud. We were walking the wetlands, you know."

I wiggled my toes that were in my soaked boots. "Tell me about it."

"Bigfoot?" Tammy asked. "Sounds like you two have been taking a nip off Granny's jug. I didn't see any Bigfoot."

I knew where Tammy was going with this. "Exactly. I can't believe these two actually believe that Bigfoot exists. He's a myth around these parts," I winked.

"You saw him the same as us," Peyton bellowed. "I know you did. Why else would you run off like that?"

"Besides the fact that you two were planning to kill us, you mean?"

Brent's eyes were wide as Peyton's. "We'll be happy to surrender if you just get us out of these woods."

I had the satisfaction of hearing them grovel firsthand. That's a win-win in my book, but I'll save the victory dance until we're out of these blasted woods. "They killed Billy Matlin," I told Curt and Curtis. The Hill boys jerked Brent and Payton up by the scuff of their necks. "Does anyone have a working phone? We'd better get Sheriff Peterson out here. I hate the thought of Billy's body being way out here. I just can't believe they killed him."

"I never intentionally killed him," Peyton said. "It was all an accident."

"Tell it to the sheriff when you see him."

Curtis made the call with his satellite radio and about an hour later we heard Andrew call out, "Agnes, where in tarnation are you?"

I met him halfway as he cleared the trees with a sea of deputies and troopers led by Sheriff Peterson and Trooper Sales.

Andrew hugged me tight and I wept into his neck. I then told the sheriff where Billy's body was and how we had discovered it, only then to be confronted by Brent and Peyton who had planned to drown us in the river. Before anyone could stop him, Andrew punched Brent in the mouth, sending him flying to the ground. When he didn't move, I figured he had been knocked out.

"That'll be enough of that," the sheriff said. He spied Curt and Curtis and asked, "How do they play into this whole scenario?"

"Actually, they helped us, and Brent and Peyton gave themselves up talking like a couple of lunatics."

"Yeah," Eleanor said with her thumbs hooked into her pant loops. "They claimed that Bigfoot tried to kill them. Can you imagine? Bigfoot."

"The other contestants on the show were locked below ground of one of the cabins back at the hunting camp," I added.

Peterson spouted off orders, and two deputies went off into the woods to check out the hunting cabin for survivors.

"How did you find this cabin?" Trooper Sales asked.

"We were looking for the other people from the reality show. The camp was quite a mess and we thought they might need help."

"Agnes," Andrew spat. "Why didn't you just go back and call in the cops?"

"It seemed like a good idea at the time I guess."

"I swear, one day you're gonna get yourself killed for sure."

"I have to agree with Andrew. You should have called in the Calvary," Sheriff Peterson said.

Eleanor and I trembled. "H-How long do we have to stay here? We're soaked to our gills," I said.

"Or our feet are, at least," Eleanor added.

"What about us?" whined Peyton. "We're soaked, too. Bigfoot knocked us in the muck."

I rolled my eyes. "There they go again with their Bigfoot stories. Some people just never quit. They told us they have a fur suit and they're the ones who terrorized me the other night and had you busy all night long, Sheriff."

He nodded. "Thanks. Andrew, go ahead and take the ladies back. We'll be in touch, unless you can think of anything else you haven't told us."

"Not that I can recall right now. Besides that, those two had planned to provide bogus evidence to prove Bigfoot actually exists, which would give them twenty-five percent of the ten million dollar prize offered."

Peterson frowned. "So basically, this is all over greed? It's a senseless loss of life. Billy didn't deserve to die, and Tawas doesn't need this kind of trouble. We run a clean town here."

Trooper Sales gave me a quick hug. "Go on home now. I'd hate for my daughter to grow up without her eccentric great-grandmother."

We left, all of us weary to the bone. We told Andrew what really happened and that Bigfoot had really saved our lives, with Curt and Curtis coming in at the last moment. We made a pact to never admit that we'd seen anything even close to Bigfoot. It was in the best interest of all the residents in and around East Tawas.

Epilogue

We gathered at Eleanor's house for our after-case wrap-up gathering that had become the norm for us now. Andrew and I hadn't talked about what had happened out in the woods, which was fine by me. He had eased up complaining about my investigative activities and we were in a much better place. We still hadn't set a wedding date, but neither had Eleanor and Mr. Wilson, who happened to be currently dancing to tunes only he heard, swiveling his roller walker. Eleanor's sister, Margarita, was tapping her foot in time to the movements of Wilson, earning her a dirty look from Eleanor, but lord knows Wilson only had eyes for Eleanor. Tammy and Dixie were here, too. They were arm wrestling. It's not something I'm used to seeing women do, but as I've learned, Tammy is just not your run-of-the-mill woman. She's strong and smart as a whip. It's no wonder she managed to solve a murder case back in Bear Paw. Tammy and Dixie had been hanging out with the Hill boys of late, but it was an agreement between them that they'd just remain friends. Of course, it might have had to do with Tammy beating both of the Hill boys at their self-imposed archery competition.

When Sophia walked in the door with Trooper Sales, Bill gave them each a hug, stealing away baby Andrea whom I have rocked on my hip since she was about six months old. Sheriff Peterson strolled on the deck with the DNR and U.S. Fish and Wildlife service. Derek smiled over at Bernadette Huntington, who I heard he had started dating recently. How that was going to work out I had no idea, but at least he had quit drinking. Derek's partner, Patrick, cleared his throat. "The DNR and U.S. Fish and Wildlife Service have come to a mutual agreement to reveal the DNA analysis done from the Matlin place. Go ahead, Special Agent Dillard, since you were in charge of the analysis."

"Go ahead. You DNR guys are quite capable of reading the results since this was a joint effort, even though we had a bumpy start."

"Thanks, Duane." He cleared his throat. "In the matter of the samples found at the Matlin place, it has been determined that the hair and animal scat found was from an undetermined source."

"What does that mean?" I asked.

"It's an unknown species. We cross-matched it, but just couldn't find anything that closely resembles it."

"So, it could be Bigfoot?" Eleanor asked with a shake of her head.

Sheriff Peterson chuckled. "Please don't open that can of worms again. All of the Bigfoot sightings have ceased to come into dispatch."

"No more Bigfoot?" I asked. "What about all those big game hunters?"

"We have prevented any of them from causing any real harm. They have all since left town. I think they were just curious for the most part."

"And what about Billy Matlin's death?"

"He choked to death. We're not sure if it was accidental, but both Brent and Peyton have been charged with murder. They pled guilty fairly quickly. Their only request was to serve their time far from Northern Michigan."

"They still are trying to claim Bigfoot attacked them?"

"Yes, but nobody believes them and they both passed the psych exam. We had quite a bit of evidence on them since your microphone was running the whole time. It was stored on Pierre DePaul's hard drive as part of the show."

"Like an automatic transmission."

"Yes. He's still going on with the show, deleting some content and announcing that Brent and Peyton had a breakdown after seeing Bigfoot firsthand."

"I suppose he'd have to say something. I can't wait for the show to broadcast. We'll be celebrities."

We all took a drink of the wine that my daughter Martha brought us, and toasted to the imaginary Bigfoot, who I still continued to feed in a pizza box out in the woods. After all, he did save my life. Sure, the sightings had ceased to be reported, but I figure most folks around the Tawas area don't mind so much that Bigfoot lives amongst them and neither did I, provided he stays deep in the wetlands and out of sight.

Interested in learning more about Margarita, Tammy and Dixie, check out Target of Death, A Cajun Cooking Mystery.

Excerpt from Target of Death

Chapter One

Well, congrats, Tammy. We are officially in the middle of nowhere." I wrinkled my brow in irritation. "Not at all." I rustled the map in my lap. "I think we're almost there."

Dixie rolled her eyes. "You said that an hour ago."

"Remind me again why I brought you?"

"Because I'm your bestest friend in the world and you'd be lost without me."

I smiled. How couldn't I smile when Dixie said something that sweet? Most folks might think Dixie is an airhead on account of how her blonde hair was all teased and big, but she's one of the smartest women I know—after me, that is. I had to chuckle at that. Seriously, though, I'm Tammy Lynn Rodrigue and I'm anything but the smartest woman on the planet. I quit using my real last name years ago to hide my family's dark past. I'm from Estelle, Louisiana, and I was heading to Michigan to attend an archery competition, The Tournament of Trouble, in Bear Paw, Michigan. That is, if I ever found the place. Since I recently lost my job, I really need the prize money to keep a roof over my head and food in my belly. Oh, and did I mention that it was in the dead of winter? So much for wearing my flip-flops.

"It sure is snowing hard," Dixie announced.

"I can see that. I sure hope we don't —"

"Uh-oh. I so know you're not finishing that sentence. It's bad luck and you know it."

"There is no such thing as bad luck," I said, while crossing myself like Grandma always taught me to do—when she wasn't going to church every dang day, that is. Since I wasn't all that much of a Jesus freak, I rubbed my antler pendant that was attached around a black cord necklace for good measure. It was made from the antler of the first deer I ever killed with an arrow. I killed it on the first try, too. That made my dad pretty proud. Mama wasn't too happy about it, though. She thought I should do more ladylike things, such as knitting. She kinda gave up after awhile, which made me happy. But it's not like I'm all that much of a tomboy since every once in a while, I do like to dress up in pink, with green glitter eye shadow to accent my hazel eyes and red hair. I also love to wear heels on occasion, preferably in the form of leather boots, even though I much prefer the chunky heel type. They've come in handy a few times, too, like when a date got out of line. Oh yes, these boots were so made for walking all over you.

Dixie looked over at me and busted out laughing. "You crack me up, Tammy."

"Why, now," I said, acting like I hadn't just looked like I was superstitious as all get out.

"Slow down, would you," Dixie shouted, but it was too late as the Dodge Dart I was driving slid sideways, narrowly missing a truck. The car spun around into a donut, landing smack in a ditch with a thump.

I pressed my hand against my chest as my heart hammered away and glared at Dixie like it was her fault. "Well, so much for good luck charms."

"All that crossing yourself didn't do anything for you, either, but it sure was funny."

It was snowing so hard now that I couldn't see much at all. "I told you to rent a four-wheel drive truck!"

"I tried, but they didn't have any."

Dixie and I crawled out of the car, still arguing, when the truck I almost nailed also stopped. A tall man hopped out and proceeded to pull out chains from the bed of his truck, then walked toward us.

Not one to be intimidated, even though I was in unfamiliar territory, I stood my ground, trying to look all brave. It really wasn't an act. My dad always told me never let them see you sweat. I wasn't actually sweating, but I was possibly perspiring a little. I'm so blaming that on the near-death experience I just had, or thought I had, anyway.

The man was covered from head to toe with a feather-down jacket and snow pants. He never said a word as he hooked the chain around the undercarriage of my rental car. It was hard to see what he even looked like since he had a ski mask covering his entire face. Under other circumstances, I'd have worried about a man in a ski mask, but then again, I was from Louisiana and I was used to seeing people in masks during Mari Gras in New Orleans. Plus, it was quite cold and neither Dixie nor I were prepared for it, jacket-wise.

Finally, the man stood up and yelled, "Get behind the wheel and I'll get you out of there. All you have to do is help steer the car."

I wanted to say, "Hey, buddy, tell me something I don't know," but he was being neighborly, so the least I could do was be nice and act all frail. Hey, if it helped me get the car back on the road, I was game.

I crawled back in the car and started the engine, gripping the steering wheel hard as the car jerked when the chain tightened against it. The engine of the truck roared, and the car was easily pulled from the ditch. My feet pounded the floorboard in my version of a happy dance. I watched as the man moved from his truck and removed the chains. I got out and thanked him.

"You sure talk funny," he said, referring to my Louisiana accent, no doubt.

"So do you," I fired back.

"Are you Louisiana Sassy, by chance?"

I put my hands on my hips. "What if I am?"

He laughed. "Of all the luck. You have quite a reputation."

I didn't like that a bit, but before I had a chance to teach this Michigan man a lesson about how to treat a lady, Dixie said, "She sure does. She's deadly with a bow. We're here for the archery competition."

"Well, you might just want to turn around now because I'm going to win that competition. I'm not about to let a girl one-up me."

"I see," I began. "I have been beating men in competitions for years and I'll have no problem defeating you. Louisiana Sassy doesn't take any guff from anyone, least of all a man wearing a ski mask."

He swiped the ski mask off, flashing me his cat-green eyes. A smile curved his lips. "It's so on, little lady, but I hope you brought plenty of tissue for when you lose to me. I'm a national champ. I've never been beat."

I leaned forward until I was eye-to-eye with the man. "Me, either."

He eyed my car. "You can't even seem to stay out of a ditch."

"Oh, that little thing. Back home we have bigger potholes."

"Is that right? Well, you certainly couldn't have drove yourself out of the itty bitty ditch," he laughed. "You better move along now before you catch yourself a cold. This isn't Louisiana. If you plan to last long enough to enter the competition, you better buy yourself a parka. It's going to be in the twenties tonight."

Our conversation was interrupted as flashing lights illuminated through a cluster of pine trees further up the road. As the cop cars screeched to a stop, I bit my lower lip. Was this standard policy in Michigan when a car goes in a ditch? I then shook my head, as that didn't make a lick of sense since I had never even called a wrecker. Something was wrong; I could just feel it in my bones.

Cops staggered from their cars that had careened down on us only moments ago. One of the cops froze when he scrutinized the man who had pulled us out. "What's going on here, Daniel?"

"I was just helping these ladies out of a ditch."

There was something about how he said 'ladies' that I hated, but then again, I was surprised someone from the north even knew what a lady was.

"Is there something wrong?" I asked the trooper, noting the state police emblem on his car.

"Yes, we found a dead guy in a wooded area not far from here."

"Oh, my," Dixie said. "That's just awful."

Daniel waved his hands. "Don't look at me. I just got here. I can't say the same for the women here. For all I know, they might be responsible."

Dixie had to hold me back before I smacked this fool. "You just pulled us out of the ditch—or have you forgotten?"

"We take murder investigations seriously here, and as such, we have enough probable cause to search your vehicles," the trooper informed us.

I pointed in the direction of my rental car. "Knock yourself out, but I'm warning you, our gear is packed tightly in the car."

Daniel was stone-faced for the moment as he surveyed the cops going through his truck. I, on the other hand, was livid as I helplessly watched as the cops toss our belongings on the ground. "Hey," I shouted. "Take it easy, would ya."

When they removed my bow, I rushed forward. "Don't you dare throw that on the ground. I need that for the competition."

"Where are you from, Miss?"

"Estelle, Louisiana. Why?"

"I was trying to identify your accent." He allowed me to hold the bow, but when he came back with an arrow, he frowned. "Have you been bow hunting today?"

"No, I hardly think it's bow season in January."

"Even if it was," Dixie said, "we're from out of state."

"Good point." He waved the other cops forward. "This arrow looks similar to the one we found in the victim."

"How is that?"

"It also had white and pink feathers."

"You mean fletches, don't you? You obviously know nothing about archery, and I imagine arrows like that can be found anywhere." I gave him a hard stare. "There is an archery competition in Bear Paw, don't forget."

"I know all about it, young lady," a man behind me said. "I'm Sheriff Simon Price. We'll be taking your arrow to compare it to the one used in the crime."

I stared at the silver-haired sheriff with less than enthusiasm. "I see. Well, we just got here, so surely we can't be suspects and you'll find my arrows all have field tips, which are used for tournaments. Whoever killed the victim must have used a broad-head tip. That's what most hunters use."

"You can check our GPS unit in the car if you'd like," Dixie volunteered. "It will prove that we just got here."

"I see. Well, like I said, we'll be retaining the arrow. I hope you ladies plan on sticking around in town until the investigation is cleared up." He stroked his mustache. "I have a friend in town who could offer you a place to stay while you're here. Margarita Hickey, she owns the local restaurant, Hidden Pass."

I sighed. "Sure, whatever you say."

The sheriff then gave me directions, which I only half listened to. How hard could it be to find? My thoughts were more on Daniel, who seemed to have some kind of death wish for suggesting Dixie or I could be capable of murder. Oh, I have had dark thoughts, all right, but it's not something I'd ever act on. My family already had a black mark against it and didn't need another.

The cops left our belongings on the snow-covered ground and I just wanted to scream at them to put everything back the way they found it, but I knew that would be impossible on account of how hard it was for Dixie and me to pack the car the first time around. I had some harsh words for that Daniel character, but he had piled into his truck and sped off.

As the sheriff made for his car, I asked, "Can you give me the full name of the man who helped us out of the ditch? I haven't properly thanked him for helping us out."

"Daniel Adams. He's our local archery champ. I'm fairly certain that he won't let a woman beat him."

Oh, I'd like to beat Daniel, all right. Instead, I just nodded in agreement. "I'm so used to the type, and it's always so gratifying to me when I—"

"Meet them later for a congratulatory drink," Dixie interjected.

Dang that Dixie for interrupting me before I could add that I'd kick that man's ass all the way to China. I suppose I should thank Dixie. Otherwise, we might not run into him again until the competition, and that just wouldn't do. For all I knew, the Daniel character might be the one responsible for the murder, although it didn't appear that the cops had found any bow or arrows in his truck, but he sure lit outta here fast.

USA Today Bestseller Madison Johns

When independent writer Madison Johns began writing at the age of forty-four, she never imagined she'd have two books in her Agnes Barton Senior Sleuths mystery series make it onto the USA Today Bestsellers list. Sure, these books are Amazon bestsellers, but USA Today?

Although sleep-deprived from working third shift, she knew if she used what she had learned while caring for senior citizens to good use, it would result in something quite unique. The Agnes Barton Senior Sleuths mystery series has forever changed Madison's life, with each of the books making it onto the Amazon bestseller's list for cozy mystery and humor.

Madison is a member of Sisters In Crime. Madison is now able to do what she loves best and work from home as a full-time writer. She has two children, a black lab, and a hilarious Jackson Chameleon to keep her company while she churns out more Agnes Barton stories with a few others brewing in the pot.

http://madisonjohns.com

Sign up for Madison's newsletter
https://www.facebook.com/MadisonJohnsAuthor/
app_100265896690345

88445903R00117

Made in the USA
Middletown, DE
09 September 2018